THIS RIVERI
CONT~~~~
FULL-LENGTH NOVELS:

Tour Troubles
— and —
Betty Cooper, Baseball Star

Other titles in the Riverdale High series:

Tour Troubles

Michael J. Pellowski
Art by Stan Goldberg

Hyperion Paperbacks

First Edition

1 3 5 7 9 10 8 6 4 2

Library of Congress Catalog Card Number: 91-58616
ISBN: 1-56282-192-X

Chapter 1

"Hold it! Hold it!" I cried. I put down my guitar and waved my hands in the air. The rest of the band abruptly quit playing their instruments, too.

"What is it *now*, Archie?" Reggie Mantle, our bass guitarist, asked—or, rather, grumbled. "We're never going to get through this rehearsal if you stop the music for every little thing."

I took a deep breath and looked around our practice space, my garage. I glanced at Veronica Lodge, on keyboard, and then at Jughead Jones, on the drums. "It just wasn't right," I explained.

"Archiekins," Veronica cried angrily, banging her hand on her keyboard. "What do you mean, it wasn't right? It sounded perfect to me!"

"That's just it," I answered Veronica, or Ronnie, as everyone called her. "It was okay, but it *wasn't* perfect."

Reggie and Ronnie gritted their teeth and exchanged angry glances.

"I know it's getting late and you're tired," I continued, "but if The Archies are ever going to get anywhere in the music business, we have to rehearse each number until we get it down pat."

"Tired?" grunted Veronica. "Hmph!" There was fire in her eyes. "The Archies have been playing together for years, and we haven't gone anywhere yet. I'm tired, all right. I'm tired of playing completely uncool clubs. I'm tired of rehearsing every Tuesday, Thursday, and Sunday night in your smelly old garage. And I'm tired of waiting for a break that never comes!"

Veronica was the temperamental type. I guess her impatience over our prolonged lack of success stemmed from the fact that she was the daughter of the richest man in our hometown of Riverdale. She wasn't accustomed to not having her every wish promptly fulfilled. Whatever Veronica wanted, her father gave her. But joining my band hadn't made her the instant celebrity she'd wanted to become. Even though The Archies had enjoyed some success on a local level, we were still hoping for that one big break in the music business.

"Stop acting like a child, Ron," Betty Cooper, who played tambourine, told Veronica.

Veronica folded her arms across her chest and, with a flick of her chin, whipped her silky black hair from her shoulders. "I am not acting like a child, Betty Cooper," she replied curtly. "Every word I've said is true. If you weren't so infatuated with Archie, you'd see that."

"*Me*, infatuated with Archie?" Betty grunted. "At least I don't moan and groan every time we have to redo a number."

Oh no, I thought. Here we go again. Because I date both Betty and Veronica on a regular basis, they are always arguing about which of them I like better. The truth is, I like them both.

"At least I'm more than just a tambourine-toting, stage-strutting backup singer," Veronica shouted. "At least I make a real contribution to the band's music."

"Listen, you keyboard-playing klutz," Betty fired back. "At least I can sing better than a tone-deaf frog."

"Girls! Knock it off!" I shouted. "If I didn't know better, I'd think you were the worst of enemies instead of the best of friends." In truth, Betty and Ronnie are tried-and-true friends who are always there for each other when the chips are down. However, when it comes to me, their competitive sides take over.

"If everyone is going to argue, I'm going into the house to ask Archie's mom for a snack," Jughead said, getting up from behind his drums.

"Oh no you don't," I shouted. Jughead has the biggest appetite in Riverdale—maybe the world. If he got to my refrigerator, we'd never finish rehearsing. "Sit down!"

"See, Ron," teased Reggie. "This band *is* going places. Jug is going to Archie's kitchen for a snack, and you want to go home."

"That's it!" I shouted. "I'm tired of all of this complaining."

The garage suddenly became silent. Everyone turned to look at me.

"Anyone who no longer wants to be a member of this band can leave now." I paused and took a deep breath. "And good riddance. Maybe I'll just go solo from now on."

Ronnie smiled meekly. "I guess I lost it for a minute," she apologized. "I really like being a member of The Archies. It's just that . . . well . . . we haven't had a good gig in a long time, and that depresses me."

Betty nodded at Ron. "I know what you mean," she agreed. "Our last gig was that birthday party for a thirteen year old."

"Stop complaining," Jughead said. "We were lucky my aunt hired us for that. My cousin actually wanted a heavy metal group. And at least we all got free food." He glared in my direction. "It wasn't like that gig we played at the Elks Lodge. We even had to pay for the sodas we drank there."

"The point is," Reggie remarked, "summer's already here, and if we don't line up some steady work soon, I'm going to have to hang up my guitar and hunt for a real job." Reggie shook his head. "I agreed to keep my calendar clear so we could work on our music over summer vacation, but the key word is *work*. I expected some regular gigs at the Teen Machine Dance Club or a place like that." A lot of the best bands in the area played at the Teen Machine, a local hot spot. Several years ago a band called Street Pack had been discovered there by a record company scout. Street Pack and its leader, Jimmy Street, had gone on to the big time—albums and music videos.

"It's not easy," I confessed to Reggie. "I went to

4

see Mr. Jenkins, the manager of Teen Machine, as soon as school ended."

"And what did he say?" Betty asked anxiously.

"He liked our demos," I answered, "but he didn't have anything open. All of his dates were booked and he'd already hired a heavy metal group called Snake Bite as his house band for the summer."

"I've heard of Snake Bite," Reggie said. "They're a bit off the wall."

"What heavy metal group isn't?" Ronnie chuckled.

"Mr. Jenkins promised he would call me if anything came up," I added.

Betty smiled and shook her tambourine in the air. "I wouldn't mind playing at Teen Machine," she fantasized. "Who knows? We might even be discovered. The Archies could be the next Street Pack."

Ron smiled. "I wouldn't mind, either," she said. "I saw Jimmy Street's new video on TV last night. It was awesome. Making music videos must be lots of fun."

Reggie grinned from ear to ear. "I could live with being a rock star," he said dreamily. "Just think of the beautiful groupies. I could have a new date every night of the week."

Suddenly Jug whacked his cymbals. We all jumped. Jug exhaled and straightened the pointed hat he always wore. "If you're going to talk forever, I'm going out for that bite to eat."

"No! No! We're playing right now," I said firmly. I checked my guitar. "Let's try 'Riverdale Rock.' "

"Riverdale Rock" was a piece I'd written for our

group. We'd been trying to get the kinks out of it for months.

"Kick it!" I said as I began to count off for the band. We began to play. As usual, I sang lead, backed up by the girls and Reggie. We cranked it up.

"Riverdale rock! Rock! Rock!" I sang as we finished the song.

"Rock, rock, rock," Betty and Ron repeated softly, letting their voices fade away. With a final chord on the guitar, Reggie and I finished playing.

"Very nice," someone said, applauding. We turned to see my mom standing at the garage door. "That was very nice, indeed."

"Thanks, Mrs. Andrews," said Jughead. "But you're prejudiced. You've always been our biggest fan."

Jughead was right. Mom had encouraged and helped us from Day One. She was a combination stage mom and roadie. In fact, it was my mom who had really turned me on to music. Before she met my father, Mom had sung lead with an all-girl group. They might even have had a chance at the big time if they hadn't broken up to attend college.

"I don't want to intrude," my mom said, "but if you're finished rehearsing, I made a plate of sandwiches. I thought you might be hungry."

"Now you're talking," Jughead said. He shot up out of his seat.

"And you, Mr. Lead Singer," Mom said, pointing at me, "have a phone call."

"I do?" I asked. "Who is it?"

"He said his name is Pete Jenkins," Mom told me.

We all put our instruments away and headed toward the house.

"Mr. Jenkins, the manager of the Teen Machine Dance Club?" I exclaimed, my eyes widening in surprise. "What can he want?"

Chapter 2

"These sandwiches are super," I heard Jug say as I walked back into the kitchen after getting off the phone with Mr. Jenkins.

"Don't be bashful, Jug," said Mom. "Help yourself to as many as you want."

"I don't have to be told twice," Jug said. He eagerly reached out and snatched two more sandwiches from the platter.

"Does anyone want more lemonade?" my mom asked.

"No thanks, Mrs. Andrews," Reg said as I walked toward the table.

"Hi, Son," Mom said. "I was just about to bring you some lemonade."

"Thanks." I accepted the glass from her and took a long drink. When I lowered the glass, I noticed that everyone at the table had stopped eating and was staring at me. Well, actually Jughead was staring but still eating, too.

"Well?" Betty prodded.

"Well, what?" I said, pretending I didn't know what she was asking.

"That was Mr. Jenkins, the manager of the Teen Machine Dance Club, wasn't it?" Reggie asked.

I nodded. I pulled out a chair from the table and lowered myself into it.

"Spit it out, Archie, and stop grinning like the cat who just swallowed the canary," Ron ordered.

I smiled at my friends. I couldn't hold back the news one second longer. "He offered us a job playing at the Teen Machine."

"*Yahoo!*" Reggie shouted, throwing his arms into the air.

"Yes!" Betty said. She thrust a fist skyward in a display of triumph.

"At last," Ronnie remarked.

"Congratulations," said my mom.

"What does it pay?" Jug asked.

I leaned back in my chair. My smile faded just a bit. "Well," I sputtered, "we get paid, but we don't get paid much."

"What do you mean we don't get paid much?" Reggie demanded. "This sounds fishy to me."

I took a deep breath. "Here's the deal," I said, leaning forward and resting my arms on the table. "On Friday night, the Teen Machine is having a battle of the bands. There are four local bands involved, including the house band. It's a competition. Each competing band gets fifty dollars."

"Fifty bucks!" groaned Reggie. He slapped his forehead with his palm. "Here I thought this was our big break, and we're getting a lousy fifty bucks."

"Hey! That's a whole ten bucks apiece," Ron said sarcastically.

"I'm not finished," I interrupted. "The winner of the contest, which is decided by the audience, gets an additional five hundred dollars."

Reggie's eyes widened. "Five hundred smackers! Now that's more like it."

"Definitely," Ronnie agreed, nibbling on her sandwich.

"Don't count your chickens before they hatch," cautioned Betty soberly. Betty was not only beautiful and talented but also levelheaded. "There's no guarantee we'll win. After all, we have only a week to prepare for the contest, right, Archie?" She looked at me.

I fidgeted in my seat and didn't answer.

"Right?" she said again.

I shrugged. "Not exactly," I mumbled.

"But you said the competition is on Friday," Betty said.

"This Friday," I answered in a voice just above a whisper.

"You mean tomorrow?" Reggie sputtered in disbelief.

I raised my eyebrows and nodded. "One of the bands canceled at the last minute, and Mr. Jenkins called to ask me if The Archies would go on instead. I told him we'd be glad to."

"Oh, great," lamented Reggie. "We weren't even one of his first choices. He calls at the last minute and expects us to jump at the chance to play at his crummy club. He must think we're really desperate or something."

"We are," Jughead said, breaking into the conversation for the first time. He looked around the table. "Does anyone want that last sandwich?" After we'd all shaken our heads, Jug plucked the sandwich off the plate. "I don't see what the problem is here," he said, between bites. "We need a break, and this could be it. Who knows? We could end up the champs!"

"Juggie is right," Betty agreed. "Let's stop looking a gift horse in the mouth." Betty looked in my direction "What bands would be competing against us, Archie?"

"Like I told you in the garage, the house band is Snake Bite," I replied. "Then there's an all-girl group called Lola and the Cola Girls, and a rap group named T. C. Slammer and the Rapmasters."

"We can beat all of them with some good old-fashioned rock and roll," Betty said, smiling. She leaned back in her chair. "And after we win the battle of the bands, we'll be on the road to success," she predicted.

"That's the spirit," my mom put in.

"But what songs are we going to play?" Reggie asked. "What about rehearsing? We can't just go out onstage stone cold."

"Why not?" Jug said. He smiled at Reggie. "A gig like this is perfect for you, Reg. Going onstage stone cold should be easy for a musician who has rocks in his head."

We all laughed, even my mom.

Reggie growled in response. He was used to Jug's insults.

"Relax, Reg," Betty said. "Let Archie make the decisions. After all, he's our leader."

"That's fine with me," Jug said.

"Me, too," Ronnie agreed.

"Me, three," Reggie said reluctantly.

"Thanks, everyone," I acknowledged, "but if we're

going to be a successful group, we have to work together on every aspect of our performance. We can
all decide what songs to do. After all, we can't let
egos get in the way. I think we'll need lots more
sandwiches, Mom," I said. "If we're going to win
that competition tomorrow night, we'll have to go
back to the garage and rehearse." I looked around
the table. "Right, guys?" I asked.

"Right," Reggie said, standing up. "Let's go."

"Follow me," I said, getting to my feet. I started
for the door and accidentally tripped over the leg of
my chair. I almost fell flat on my face.

"We haven't won the contest yet, and Archie is
already on a road trip," Reggie cracked. He was always ready with a wise remark.

"Very funny," I said, steadying myself. "But you're
right. If we win this contest, we just might end up
on the road. We might even go on a world tour."

"Yeah! We can start our tour in the world-famous
Andrewses' garage," Jughead said.

"Hey, Arch," Reg said as we all filed out of the
house and into the garage. "Why don't we play 'Riverdale Rock' at the contest? We've never tried it before."

I shook my head. "I don't think that's a good idea,
Reg," I answered. " 'Riverdale Rock' isn't ready to
go yet." I pointed at my heart. "I'll know in here
when we're ready to perform 'Riverdale Rock' in
front of an audience."

"Archie's right," Betty agreed. Ron nodded her
approval, too.

"Stop gabbing and let's rehearse," Jug called to

13

us. "It's late. We've got a lot of work to do before tomorrow night."

Reg and I walked over and picked up our guitars. We strapped them on and plugged into our amplifiers.

"Okay," I said, "let's rock the house!"

"You mean the garage," Betty corrected.

Chapter 3

I peeked out from backstage. The Teen Machine was crammed to capacity. Young people were packed on the dance floor like sardines to hear and judge the battle of the bands.

"Now, tell me again how this contest works?" Betty asked as she walked up beside me. We stood in the wings waiting for our turn to perform, along with our competitors. I turned to look at Betty.

"Each band performs alone at first," I began, explaining the rules of the contest. "After all four bands finish playing, the audience votes for its favorite two bands. Then those two bands face off against each other. They take turns playing songs, one after another, in a sort of musical showdown. When they're finished, everyone votes again. The winner takes home five hundred dollars."

"I sure hope that's us," Betty sighed, glancing around. "Those other bands look pretty good. Lola and the Cola Girls are sure to turn some heads in those outfits, and those four guys in Snake Bite are totally intimidating."

I had to admit that Lola and the Cola Girls looked really cool in their bright red minidresses and red stockings. Reggie was so thunderstruck by Lola, the lead singer, that he'd been following her around ever since we'd arrived to set up. Unfortunately for Reggie, Lola kept giving him the cold shoulder.

"Don't let those guys in Snake Bite scare you just because they dress in leather," I advised Betty.

Betty shuddered. "Oh, right," she replied. "Tell me that the guy with the spiked hair and the earring in his nose doesn't send chills down your spine, Archie!"

"I admit that he looks tough," I confessed, "but what kind of drummer is he? As far as I'm concerned, he can't hold a candle to Jughead. The only guy in that group who can really jam is their lead guitarist, Gunny Witherspoon."

"Hmph!" said Betty. "Gunny can play, but he's a total creep! He thinks he's the best guitarist in the world. What an ego!"

I nodded. "I guess he feels superior because he's been playing longer than anyone else in the competition. I heard Mr. Jenkins say he's twenty-two years old."

"If he doesn't keep away from me, he may not make it to twenty-three," Betty vowed, raising her fist in the air. "He thinks every girl is madly in love with him."

I shrugged. "It takes all kinds." I glanced around. "What do you think of the rap group?"

"T. C. Slammer seems like a nice guy, but I think his group is the weakest one here," Betty said. "You heard them during the warm-ups. They don't seem to work together well."

16

"Speaking of that," I said, "we'd better check on the rest of our group." Betty and I passed the other bands as we walked toward Reg, Ron, and Jug.

"Is that geek from The Archies still pestering you for a date?" we overheard one of the Cola Girls ask Lola.

"Yeah! That dork won't take no for an answer," Lola said as we moved past her group. Betty and I snickered. As we walked further backstage, we found Gunny Witherspoon leaning against the wall near Snake Bite's dressing room. The house band had the club's only dressing room.

"Yo!" Gunny called to me. "If it isn't Archie himself and his stuck-up tambourine player." Betty and I stopped.

"Yeah?" I replied. "What do you want?"

"Don't you think you should get dressed for the contest?" he asked. I glanced at Betty. Our band wore regular street clothes to perform. I had on torn jeans, a black T-shirt, a leather vest, and a red bandana. Betty had on black tights, a short skirt, and a tank top.

"We *are* dressed," I said. I had the feeling he knew that already and was just trying to be a wise guy.

"Well, dude," Gunny mocked, "if you play as shabbily as you look, you might as well pack up and head for home now." He laughed out loud. Before I could reply, he walked into the dressing room and shut the door in my face.

"Is everything okay?" Mr. Jenkins said. He'd walked up unnoticed while I was talking to Witherspoon. "Are The Archies ready to rock?" he asked.

17

"Yes, sir," I said. Betty smiled and nodded.

"Good," he said. "I'm about to kick off this competition, so get your group together in the wings while I introduce Lola and her gals." Mr. Jenkins turned and walked away.

"It's show time," Betty said. We were scheduled to go on second, between Lola and the Cola Girls and T. C. Slammer and the Rapmasters. The house band, Snake Bite, was on last. We moved down the hall. At its end, near a fire exit, we found Ron, Reg, and Jug. Ronnie was sitting on a chair. Jug was slumped on the floor, his drumsticks clutched in his hand and his pointy hat tilted down over his eyes. Reggie was leaning against a wall, as was his bass guitar.

"Where have you two been?" Ron asked.

"Checking out the house," I replied. "Let's collect our stuff. Mr. Jenkins is about to introduce the first group."

"It's about time," Jug said, getting to his feet. He picked up a huge lunch box on the floor near him. Jug always brought along a big backstage snack to tide him over on our gigs.

"Is there anything left in there?" I joked.

"Not much," he admitted.

"Quit the gab, and let's get ready to play," Reggie admonished. He took out his dark sunglasses and slipped them on. "I've got a feeling this is going to be a lucky night for us."

Betty giggled. "Oh, I see," she said. "Unlucky in love, lucky in music competitions, huh?"

Reggie lifted his glasses to stare at Betty, then dropped them back onto the bridge of his nose.

"Have you been talking to Lola?" he asked. "I don't care what you've heard—she begged me to go out with her, but I told her no."

Betty laughed. So did I.

"Forget Lola," I advised Reg. "All we care about now is the audience." I looked at my group. "Let's knock 'em dead, Archies!"

We started toward the stage entrance and heard Mr. Jenkins introducing Lola and the Cola Girls. The crowd roared as music began to play. T. C. Slammer and his group were waiting in the hall for their turn to perform.

"Yo! Good luck, Archies!" T. C. called out.

"Thanks, T. C.," I answered. "The same to you." We continued on until we reached the end of the long hall. We halted in the wings, beside Mr. Jenkins. We could see Lola and the Cola Girls out onstage, doing their thing. The crowd was loving every minute of it.

"They're good," Mr. Jenkins commented.

"They're too good," I heard Ron mutter under her breath.

"They *are* good," I whispered back. "But we're better."

We listened to Lola and her band blare out song after song. When they finished, the crowd was really worked up—ready to rock with us.

"Okay, Archies," said Mr. Jenkins, preparing to walk back onstage. "It's time to do your thing."

Lola and the Cola Girls threw kisses to the crowd as a round of thunderous applause echoed through the building. Then they ran offstage, and Mr. Jenkins stepped out.

"Great show," I told Lola and her girls as they went by.

When the applause started to fade, Mr. Jenkins picked up the mike. "Thanks, Lola and the Cola Girls," he said. "And now, to keep the house rocking, put your hands together for The Archies!" He motioned toward us. A spotlight lit up the secondary stage, where our equipment had been set up.

"Let's do it!" I said. I rushed out onstage, followed by Betty, Ron, Reg, and Jug. We quickly took our places and plugged into our amplifiers. The crowd quieted. When we were ready, I lifted a hand into the air and cocked my electric guitar on my hip.

"We're The Archies, and we're ready to rock!" I yelled. I pointed at the crowd. "Are you?" The crowd roared back its response. I turned to the band. "Kick it!" I hollered. Ronnie hit the keyboard and we all picked up the beat. I began to belt out the lyrics of a famous sixties song we'd arranged for ourselves. Everyone loved it. Again and again we played our hearts out, working the crowd into a frenzy. By the time we finished our last number, we had the audience in our pocket.

"We're The Archies!" I cried as I strummed my guitar one last time. "And we're out of here!"

As we unplugged, the audience raised the roof with wild cheers and appreciative applause.

"There they go," Mr. Jenkins called from the other stage as we dashed toward the wings. "Give The Archies a big hand. They were great."

"We did it," Betty exclaimed. We stepped into the hall and walked past T. C. Slammer and the Rapmasters.

"Way to rock," T. C. called as the Rapmasters hurried out onstage.

"We were great," Reggie said, removing his shades.

"The crowd loved us," Ronnie said. She hugged me and planted a big kiss on my cheek. "You were terrific."

"You know, Arch," Jug said, retrieving his lunch box from a backstage corner, "I'd say we have a really good chance of winning this contest."

I didn't answer, but I was thinking the same thing.

Chapter 4

I was too nervous to even speak as Betty, Ron, Reg, Jug, and I stood on the alternate stage, in front of a noisy audience. Lola and the Cola Girls were huddled beside us. Snake Bite and T. C. and his band stood on the other stage.

"You've heard all four of our bands and voted for your top two favorites," Mr. Jenkins said. "Now it's time to announce the finalists and continue the Teen Machine Dance Club's Battle of the Bands." Mr. Jenkins looked from one stage to the other. "You all did a super job," he complimented.

I looked at Ron and Betty. They both had their fingers crossed.

"Our two finalists," announced Mr. Jenkins, "are Snake Bite and . . . The Archies!"

"Yes!" I shouted. I turned and we each hugged one another.

"We're in the finals!" Reg exclaimed.

"Good luck," Lola said, coming over with her group to congratulate us.

"Thanks, babe," Reggie said. He smiled at Lola and wiggled his eyebrows flirtatiously. "Are you sure you don't want to leave your phone number? When

I become a big star, you can tell all your friends you once dated the famous Reggie Mantle."

"Get real," Lola said. She shook her head and walked away from us.

"I hope you guys win," T. C. Slammer shouted to us as he and his band exited the other stage.

"Thanks!" Jug answered. He waved to the Rapmasters.

The crowd was still buzzing as stagehands and security people and waiters began to set up for the next round of playing.

"For the final showdown, both bands will take turns performing," Mr. Jenkins announced. "Snake Bite will lead off."

As Mr. Jenkins went over the voting rules again, Gunny Witherspoon made his way over to me. I thought he was going to wish us luck. I should have known better.

"I don't know how you made it to the finals," he said, "but we're going to blow you away!"

"Hey, dude! What's your problem?" I snapped before he could turn his back to me. "This is just a friendly competition."

Gunny looked me squarely in the eyes and sneered. He shook his head. "There is no such thing as friendly competition in the music business, mister," he told me. "It's every man for himself. The only way for a band to get to the top is to leave the wreckage of other bands in its wake." He pointed at me menacingly. "And The Archies are headed for their first major wreck, dude!" He walked back to his band.

"That guy is a real jerk," Betty said.

"Yeah, but he's kind of cute," Ron said. We glared at her, and she quickly corrected herself. "I mean, he's cute in a weird sort of way."

"Forget that chump," Jug advised. "The stage is ready. Let's show him and his friends who's going to wreck whom." I nodded in agreement as we took our place onstage and prepared to play.

"We're ready to rock again," Mr. Jenkins called. The crowd hooted and howled. "First up is Snake Bite," he continued. "Crank it up, guys!" He lowered the mike, and spotlights hit the other stage. Snake Bite began to play a hard-hitting heavy metal song that included a long guitar solo by Gunny.

"He plays a nasty guitar, Arch," Reg whispered.

I nodded. I had to admit that Gunny was one of the best guitarists I'd ever heard. His playing mesmerized me.

Before I knew it, Mr. Jenkins was speaking to the roaring crowd again. "Now it's The Archies' turn to rock you in your socks!" he cried. Spotlights hit our stage and the lights on the other stage dimmed.

"You ain't heard nothing yet," I shouted to the crowd. "If you think that was hot, let us turn up the rock and roll thermostat for you." We began to play as if we were possessed by the spirit of rock and roll. When we finished, the club was really rocking.

Mr. Jenkins got ready to introduce Snake Bite's second number. But before he could speak, the audience began to chant. *"Archies! Archies! Archies!"* they cried, refusing to settle down. From our darkened stage, we could see Snake Bite frowning and squirming under the lights.

"We've got them right where we want them," I whispered to the band.

Finally the crowd quieted enough for Snake Bite to get into their next song. The audience gave them a good hand when they finished, but it was obvious to everyone which band had captured the crowd. By the time we had finished our second number, the outcome of the contest wasn't really in question. Our third and final song was the icing on the cake. On that particular night we were the best band in the place, and everyone knew it—even though I'm sure the members of Snake Bite wouldn't admit it. They never even waited for Mr. Jenkins to announce the official vote. Instead they slinked off the stage in disgust halfway through our last song and disappeared backstage.

"I don't have to tell you what you already know," Mr. Jenkins announced to the crowd. He waved a check for five hundred dollars in the air. "The winner of the Battle of the Bands is . . . The Archies!" As the crowd exploded into cheers and applause, Mr. Jenkins walked over to our stage and handed me the check. Jug tapped a rim shot on his drum, which made the crowd crack up.

"Bring your band back into my office in twenty minutes," Mr. Jenkins whispered in my ear. "I have someone I want you to meet."

"Sure," I said. I pocketed the check and waved to the cheering crowd. Behind me, Betty, Ron, and Reg were throwing kisses to our newfound fans. Even

Jughead, who hardly ever showed any emotion, was waving and beaming. What could possibly ever top this moment?

"What's this all about?" Betty asked as we walked toward Mr. Jenkins's office in the rear of the dance club.

"Yeah. Who do we have to meet?" Reggie said. He wasn't very happy about having to leave our adoring fans so soon. "I wasn't finished basking in the lime-light. I didn't even have enough time to get any phone numbers."

"Business before pleasure," Jughead said. He lifted an apple to his mouth and bit off a big chunk.

"All work and no play," Ronnie complained. "I was just starting to enjoy being a celebrity when you rudely pulled me away for this meeting."

"Mr. Jenkins told me to bring you guys to his office in twenty minutes, and that's what I'm doing," I replied. Our group halted in front of Mr. Jenkins's door. I knocked firmly.

"Come in," Mr. Jenkins called.

I pushed the door open and we entered the room. The office was decorated with all sorts of music memorabilia. On the wall nearest us was a large photo of Jimmy Street and the Street Pack band.

Mr. Jenkins got up from behind his desk as we walked toward him. A well-dressed middle-aged man, seated nearby, also rose.

"Archie," said Mr. Jenkins, "I asked you to come back here because a close friend of mine wanted to meet you and your group." Mr. Jenkins motioned toward the other man, who smiled to reveal perfect pearly white teeth. "This is Denny Diamond of the Diamond Music Management Agency."

"I-I'm pleased to meet you, Mr. Diamond," I stuttered, extending my arm.

Mr. Diamond shook my hand. "Please, call me Denny," he said. "Congratulations on the big win tonight. Your band really impressed me."

"Thanks," I said. I began to introduce my friends. "This is Betty Cooper, Ronnie Lodge, Reggie Mantle, and Jughead Jones." They all smiled and greeted Denny.

"Archie," said Mr. Jenkins, "Denny has a keen eye for young talent. In fact, he signed Jimmy Street's band after seeing them perform here." Mr. Jenkins pointed at Jimmy's picture on the wall. "Jimmy got his first recording contract thanks to Denny."

Denny smiled. "Jimmy and I still get together when he comes home to visit his folks in Martinsville. We're good friends," Denny said. Martinsville is a small town not far from Riverdale.

"Now *we're* impressed," Veronica said, flashing Denny a big smile. "Maybe we could get a chance to meet Jimmy Street sometime."

Denny laughed. "Who knows?" He looked at Ron closely. "Did you say your last name was Lodge?"

"That's right," Reggie answered for Ron. "She's the daughter of Hiram Lodge."

Ron elbowed Reg in the ribs. He doubled over.

"Unfortunately, music is one business my father has no interest in investing in," Ron stated.

Denny chuckled. "Don't worry, Ronnie," he said.

"I'm the one who's doing the investing." He looked us over carefully. "I'll be investing my time in The Archies—if you're interested."

My eyes widened in shock. "Y-you mean you want to sign us to a contract?" I sputtered. No one else said anything. They were dumbfounded. The only sound I heard behind me was that of Jughead chewing on his apple.

"I'm sure we can work out some sort of trial arrangement," Denny said. He took out a business card and handed it to me. "Stop by my office in Martinsville at 10:00 A.M. on Monday and we'll discuss it."

"We'll be there," Reggie blurted out. He'd recovered quickly from Ron's poke to his ribs.

"We sure will, Denny," I said. "Thanks." We shook hands again.

"Be sure to bring along at least one parent who can legally act on your behalf," Denny said.

"We will," Betty replied.

"Now go out and celebrate," Mr. Jenkins told us, as he ushered us toward the door. "You deserve it. Things like this don't happen too often. Very few bands ever get this kind of a chance."

"Yes, sir," I said. I opened the door to leave. "Thanks again."

"I'll have the other kid you want to talk to back here in a minute," I heard Mr. Jenkins say to Denny as we exited the room.

"How about that?" I exclaimed, holding up Denny Diamond's business card. "Are we on our way or what?"

"We're on our way, but you'd better give Betty the card, Arch," remarked Reggie.

"Huh? Why?"

"Because knowing what a goof you are, you'll probably lose it before Monday," Reggie kidded me.

I do have a reputation for being kind of absent-minded. I glanced at Betty. She smiled weakly. I shrugged and handed the card over. What the heck, I figured. Why chance it?

Chapter 5

"Isn't this great, Mrs. Andrews?" Betty said to my mother as we sat in Denny Diamond's reception room that Monday morning. My mom was seated between Betty and me on a leather couch. Ron, Reg, and Jug were on nearby chairs.

"Don't get too excited until we hear Mr. Diamond's offer," Mom replied.

"You're right, Mrs. Andrews," Betty said, nodding. "I shouldn't be so excited." Betty fidgeted in her seat. "But I can't help it."

My mom laughed.

"That's why you're here, Mom," I said, leaning close to her. "We get excited. You stay cool, calm, and businesslike."

Mom smiled at me. "That's exactly what I intend to do," she said firmly. She looked at the rest of the band. "I promised your parents I'd do my best to see you got a fair deal from Mr. Diamond, and I will."

I nodded. At first we'd all thought Mr. Lodge should represent us at this meeting, because of his business background. But after considering Mom's singing background, even Mr. Lodge had agreed that she was the best choice to hear Mr. Diamond's proposal.

Just then Denny Diamond's beautiful secretary called to us from her desk. "You can go in now," she said. "Mr. Diamond is off the phone."

"Thanks," said Reggie, putting on his dark sunglasses.

"Reggie," my mom said, "I think you're safe from the sun in here."

Jughead laughed. "Yeah, Reg," said Jug. "And you don't have to worry about being incognito, either. No one in the world knows who you are!"

Reggie grunted. "Yeah, but they will someday," he predicted as he removed his glasses and stuffed them into his shirt pocket.

We walked into Denny Diamond's office.

"Hi, everyone," Denny said, flashing us a big smile. "I'm sorry I kept you waiting. I had to take an important call from a record company on the West Coast."

"Denny," I said as we approached his desk, "I'd like you to meet my mother, Mary Andrews."

Mom extended an arm to Denny, and they shook hands. "I'm pleased to meet you," my mom said.

"The pleasure is all mine, Mrs. Andrews," Denny replied.

"Well, let's get down to business," Denny suggested. "You must all be anxious to hear what I have in mind for the band."

"We sure are," Reggie said.

We sat down in the chairs arranged around Denny's desk.

"I propose signing you to a trial contract," Denny began. He took a stack of contracts from a desk

drawer and handed one to my mom. "Here's how it works. I agree to book some club dates for the band, for which I receive a commission out of the money the clubs pay. I propose to start The Archies off with six more or less local appearances—Southside Glen, Hillside, Martinsville, Oak Knoll, and others." Denny looked at me and then glanced at the other members of the band. "How does that sound?"

"Fine to me," Veronica said.

"Okay by me," Jughead seconded.

"How much do we get paid?" Reggie wanted to know.

"Each club will pay seven hundred and fifty dollars," Denny answered.

"Wow!" Reggie exlaimed. He sat up straight in his chair and looked at the rest of us.

Denny held up his hands. "But you don't get all of that," he explained. "I get a third, out of which comes expenses like hotel accommodations. From your two-thirds you have to provide the band's transportation and pay for your food." He looked at Jughead. I wondered if he'd heard about Jug's monstrous appetite.

"That means the band keeps five hundred a show, netting three thousand for the mini-tour," my mom calculated. Denny nodded.

"What kind of clubs will they be appearing at?" Mom wanted to know.

"All the places are teen dance clubs that don't serve alcoholic beverages," Denny answered. "Basically they're all nice places where young people go to have fun. I've booked young bands into all of them before."

Mom finished looking over the contract. "This agreement is pretty simple," she said. "It calls for you to play at Hillside this Wednesday and at Southside Glen on Friday and Saturday." Mom paused. "You then return home for a few days. You go back on the road for three dates the following Thursday, Friday, and Saturday, finishing up in Martinsville." Mom looked at us very carefully. "At that point the agreement can be terminated—or extended—by either side."

Ron looked at my mom. "You mean, after the Martinsville concert, Denny can dump us if he wants to?"

"Or you can dump me," Denny quickly added. "It's an escape clause in case things don't work out." He smiled. "But I expect that they will. And if they do, then I'll sign you to a longer contract that will keep you busy all summer." Denny paused. "If your band turns out to be as good as I think it is, I might even be able to get a record company interested in you."

"Record company?" Betty echoed in disbelief.

"Albums," Jughead mumbled.

"Rock videos," Veronica put in enthusiastically.

"Groupies," Reggie muttered. He took out his sunglasses and put them on. "Yeah!"

Mom smiled. "I say, give it a shot!" she advised. "Three thousand dollars is nothing to sneeze at."

"But you have to pay for your own food and provide your own transportation," Denny reminded us. "Do you have a van or station wagon?"

"We have an old van we all chipped in for and bought last year," I said. "But we haven't been using it because it needs new tires."

35

"Let's use the prize money we won in the contest to get the van fixed," Betty suggested.

"Good idea," my mother agreed. "And we'll use our family station wagon, too."

"We?" said Reggie. He lifted his sunglasses to look at my mom.

"Of course," Mom answered. "I'll be going along as The Archies' chaperone. Your parents all insist."

Reggie frowned. "No one said anything about a chaperone to me," he muttered.

"Or to me, either," Ronnie lamented. "I think we're old enough to take care of ourselves."

"A chaperone is a good idea," Denny remarked. "In fact, if you'll check our contract, you'll see I insist upon a chaperone for all my underage bands."

My mother held up the contract and pointed out the chaperone clause.

"Welcome to the group, roadie," Betty said.

"Are there any other surprises we don't know about?" Reggie asked.

Mom shook her head. "I can't think of anything else."

"There is just one more thing," Denny added. "And without it, we don't have a deal."

My friends and I exchanged curious glances. "What thing?" I finally asked.

"I want you to add another member to The Archies," Denny replied.

His comment caught us completely off guard. I shook my head. "I-I don't understand," I said in confusion.

"Archie, you're a great lead singer, but your guitar

playing could be better," Denny said. "I want you to take on a lead guitarist so you can concentrate on vocals."

"I don't think Archie's playing is bad," Betty said, quickly coming to my defense.

"It's not that Archie is bad," Denny explained. "It's that the guy I have in mind is so good."

"Who is he? Where did you find him?" Reggie asked.

"I heard him the same night I heard you play," Denny answered. "His name is Gunny Witherspoon."

"Gunny Witherspoon!" I exclaimed, jumping to my feet. As I got up, I accidentally knocked a pencil cup off Denny's desk. Pencils went flying everywhere.

"Is there a problem with Gunny?" Denny asked as I began to collect the pencils that had landed on the carpet.

"There sure is," I said. I returned the pencils to their cup and placed it back on the desk. "Witherspoon would never agree to play with The Archies, anyway," I added. I sat back down. "Besides, he's already a member of Snake Bite."

Denny leaned back in his chair. "Gunny already said he would leave Snake Bite and join The Archies in a minute if it meant getting a chance at the big time."

I snorted. I recalled what Witherspoon had said about how competitive the music business was and how bands wrecked each other to get to the top. "That sounds like him, all right," I said. I looked at my friends. "We're a group," I reminded them. "It's not my decision alone. What do you guys think?"

Denny stood up. "Why don't I step out for a minute so you can discuss this in private."

"Who is this Gunny Witherspoon person?" my mom asked when Denny had left the room.

"He's a member of a heavy metal band named Snake Bite," I explained. "He *is* a great guitarist, but I don't think he'd fit into our group. He dresses like a punk and acts like a jerk, even though he's twenty-two years old."

My mother folded her arms across her chest. "I don't know what to tell you. This is one decision you'll have to make without my help."

Reggie stood up. "Denny said there's no deal without Gunny, so I say Gunny is in," he said.

"Gunny is a creep who will make nothing but trouble," Betty argued. "I want this gig as much as anyone, but adding Gunny to The Archies might be too high a price to pay. I'm against it. If we got this offer, we'll get others."

Jug shrugged. "Maybe we will, and maybe we won't."

"That's right," Ronnie said, adding her thoughts. "This might be our one and only shot at the big time. I say we go for it. How bad can it be to have Gunny in our group?"

"We could try it for two weeks," Jug suggested. "Like Denny said, there's an escape clause in the contract. If it doesn't work out, we can call it quits then."

I sighed. "Well, Betty?" I asked.

"If that's what everyone else wants," she agreed reluctantly.

My mother looked at me. "What's your final word, Son?" she asked.

"I guess we'll try it for two weeks," I agreed. "But I'm only doing this for the band. Personally I think Gunny is going to be much more trouble than he's worth."

At that moment the door to the office opened and Denny stuck his head in. "Have you made up your mind?" he asked.

"Yes," I said. "Gunny Witherspoon is now one of The Archies."

"Good." Denny entered the office. "I know you won't regret this." He walked over to his desk and handed each of us a contract. "Get these signed by your parents and returned to me by tomorrow," he instructed. "When you drop them off, I'll give you the details of your mini-tour." He smiled. "On Wednesday you go on the road for the first time. And make sure you get tires for that van."

"We will," I assured Denny. "In fact, we'll do that as soon as we get back to Riverdale."

"Fine," Denny said. "I'll phone Gunny and fill him in on everything. I'll have him call you at home, Archie, to make arrangements for your departure on Wednesday."

I nodded. "We'll probably meet at my house and leave from there." We all got up. Denny and I shook hands again.

"Welcome to the Diamond Music Management Agency," Denny said, smiling broadly. "I'm sure The Archies are going to be big stars."

Chapter 6

Reggie and Jughead arrived at my house around ten o'clock that Wednesday morning to help load the band's gear into our two vehicles. We wanted to have everything packed by noon so we could hit the road by one o'clock. Our first gig was in Hillside, about a four-hour drive from Riverdale. We wanted to get there with time to spare, so I'd told everyone to show up no later than 12:30. I'd done my best to make Gunny feel welcome when we'd talked on the phone on Monday night, but he hadn't sounded too enthused about becoming a member of The Archies. He'd never even asked what music the band would be playing or what we expected from our lead guitarist.

"Are you taking all of our musical arrangements?" Jug asked as he carried a crate filled with sheet music to the van.

"Yeah," I answered. "I figured I'd work on some of them to pass the time on the tour. If I'm lucky I may be able to work out the kinks in 'Riverdale Rock' and a few other songs while we're on the road."

"You're the boss," Jug said. He put the crate in the back of the van, near our instruments and amplifiers. Jug stepped back from the van and examined its four new tires. "Did we have any prize money left after we bought the tires?"

I nodded. "We still have about three hundred dollars. My mom is holding it for eating expenses on the road until we get paid for our first three club dates."

"Speaking of eating," said Jug, "I hope we're going to have lunch before we leave. All this work is making me hungry." He rubbed his stomach.

"How can you be hungry?" Reggie asked. "You had breakfast at your house. You had breakfast at my house before my mom gave us a lift to Archie's. And you had another breakfast when we got here."

I looked at Jug. "We can snack out of that lunch box I saw you put in the van," I instructed. "It's filled with food, isn't it?"

Jug looked at me as if I'd said something stupid. "Of course it is," he admitted. "But that food will have to tide me over during our four-hour ride. You said we were driving nonstop to Hillside. What do you expect me to do, waste away to nothing before our first gig?"

My mom laughed. "Don't worry, Jug," she said. "I prepared two big picnic baskets of food for us to munch on during the trip. I packed sandwiches, fried chicken, and lots of other stuff."

"All right!" said Jug. "Would it be okay if I had a little pre-trip sample, Mrs. Andrews?"

"Of course," my mom answered. "Come on. The baskets are in the kitchen. I was about to bring them out anyway." She and Jughead walked off toward the house.

I checked my watch. It was ten to twelve. "It's

getting late," I said to Reggie. "I wonder where the rest of the group is." Part of my question was instantly answered. The Lodge limo pulled up in front of our house. Out popped a chauffeur. He whipped open the rear door, and Ronnie and Betty stepped out.

"Yahoo! We're here, right on time!" Ronnie shouted. She was obviously proud of the fact that, for once, she wasn't late.

"Ronnie picked me up on the way," Betty announced as we walked over to greet the girls. "My parents both had to work and couldn't get off. But they wished us luck."

"My folks send their best, too," Ron said. Her chauffeur began to unload the girls' luggage from the car.

"Thanks," I told the girls. "I wish all our parents could be here to send us off, but leaving in the middle of the week makes that tough." I thought about my dad. He had wanted to stay home from work until we left, but he couldn't.

"What's in that bag?" Reggie asked Betty. She was holding a huge brown paper bag.

"Chocolate chip cookies," Betty answered. "I baked a fresh batch for us to take along."

"Well, don't let Jug see, or he'll eat them all," Reggie said. "You know how he loves your special cookies."

"You'd better hide them in the station wagon, Betty," I agreed. "You girls will ride in the wagon with my mother. We guys will lead the way in the van."

"Right," said Betty. She started toward the wagon.

"Will you put my luggage in the car for me please, Archie?"

"Sure," I responded. "Which ones are yours?"

"The two blue ones," Betty answered. "The rest are Ron's."

I looked toward the curb, where the limo was parked. At least ten suitcases were on the sidewalk, and the chauffeur was pulling still more out of the rear of the limo. *"Ronnie!"* I yelled. "We're going on a four-day tour, not a trip around the world! You can't take all of those!"

Veronica stared at me angrily. "But I have to!" she snapped. "What do you expect me to do, wear the same clothes all day long?"

I shook my head. "We can fit only three more suitcases in the car—four at the most," I said. "So please choose the ones you need most."

"But Archiekins," Ronnie said sweetly, batting her eyes. "Couldn't you make an exception for little ol' me?"

"Save it, Veronica," Betty called. She'd just returned from the station wagon. "You can't charm Archie like that. Right, Archie?"

"Huh? Oh! Right," I replied, snapping out of a slight daze. "Three suitcases are all you can take."

"Okay! Okay!" Ron grumbled. "Take those three." She pointed out the three largest suitcases in the pile.

"Help me, Reg," I said as I began to collect the girls' luggage. I could hear Ron grumbling as we toted the bags over to the car. We packed them in the back with the other stuff. The wagon was almost full.

"I hope Gunny doesn't have a lot of stuff," Reggie

remarked. "We don't have much room left. Gunny's things will have to go in the van."

I checked my watch. It was now twenty minutes after twelve. "I wish he'd get here already," I said. "My mom wants to meet him."

"Did you give him the right directions?" Reggie asked.

"What do *you* think?"

"Well . . .," Reggie began.

"I gave him the right directions, *and* I told him the exact time to be here."

The girls joined us at the van.

"Who are you talking about?" Betty asked.

"Gunny," I fumed. "He should have been here by now. I told him we wanted to leave early."

"Don't worry so much," Reg said. "We still have some time. Let's go in the house and wait for Gunny. Besides, I could use something cold to drink."

"I'm thirsty, too," Ron said.

"Okay," I replied. "Let's wait in the house."

We went inside and found my mom and Jughead in the kitchen. Jug was munching on a fried chicken leg. Mom was packing more food into two picnic baskets on the table.

"Is everyone here and ready to go?" she asked me.

I shook my head. "Gunny hasn't shown up yet." I walked over to the fridge and took out several cans of cold soda and handed them out to my friends.

Then we all sat down to wait for Gunny. We waited and waited and waited.

"It's almost one o'clock," I said, angrily tapping the face of my wristwatch with my finger. "I told him to be here by twelve-thirty! Where is that guy?"

"Losing your temper won't get him here any faster," my mom said soothingly. "Maybe he got lost. Why don't we have something to eat while we're waiting." She opened one of the picnic baskets.

"That sounds good," Reggie agreed. "Watching Jughead snack has made me hungry."

"Me, too," Ron admitted.

"Me, three," Betty said.

"I'm not hungry," I grumbled. I got up and began to pace the kitchen floor. "Lost, huh?" I muttered to myself. "That guy is a lost cause, all right!"

Time dragged, second by second. One o'clock came and went. We decided to move to the living room, where we'd be more comfortable. The clock kept on ticking and Gunny was still unaccounted for. At one-twenty I was fit to be tied. Even my mom was getting mad.

"If I'm going to be on time, I expect everyone else to be on time, too," Ron grumbled.

"Why don't you try calling his apartment again, Arch," Reg suggested. I'd phoned Gunny's place about ten minutes earlier and gotten his answering machine.

"What's the sense in doing that?" I replied. "If he doesn't show up soon, I say we leave and let him find his own way to Hillside."

"That suits me," Jughead said. "Thanks to him, we're already cutting it pretty close. We can't afford to wait much longer."

Suddenly the doorbell rang. We all froze. "That had better be him," I said, moving to the front door.

I whipped the door open, and there stood Gunny. He was dressed in leather pants, a torn T-shirt, and boots. On the lawn near the van I saw his guitar and gear.

"Greetings, dude," Gunny said, removing his dark sunglasses. "Are we going on tour or what?"

"You were supposed to be here an hour ago!" I yelled. "It's one-thirty! We should be on the road already."

Gunny shrugged. "Sorry. The guy who dropped me off had to make a few stops along the way. You know how it is."

"No, I don't," I snapped. "All I know is that if you're going to be part of this band, you'd better be where you're supposed to be at the time you're supposed to be there."

"Hey, man," said Gunny calmly. "Chill out. Don't freak just because I'm a bit late."

"A bit!" said Jug.

"Sixty minutes isn't a bit," Betty added.

Gunny shrugged. "Look! Are we going to stand around and argue, or are we going to get started?"

"Gunny is right," my mother put in. "We can sort this out later. We'd better hit the road." She stepped forward. "Gunny, I'm Mary Andrews."

"Wow! Totally cool. I've never traveled with a middle-aged roadie before," Gunny exclaimed.

"I'm the group's chaperone," my mom corrected. She stared Gunny right in the eye. I knew that look. I'd seen it lots of times before. It was Mom's no-nonsense look.

"Well, *I* don't need a chaperone, Mary," Gunny said.

"I don't care how old or how cool you are, young man," Mom said. "I'm in charge of this group, and I call the shots! Understand, Gunther?"

"Hey," sputtered Gunny angrily. "Nobody calls me that."

We all chuckled.

"It's your real name, isn't it?" Mom said to Gunny.

Gunny gritted his teeth. "Yeah, but nobody calls me that," he repeated.

"Gunther," Jug snickered. We all laughed again.

"Get this," he said to us. "My name is Gunny, and don't you forget it."

"Okay, Gunny," I said, "let's get your stuff in the van and head for Hillside. You'll ride with us. The girls will follow in the wagon."

Gunny stormed off toward the van.

"How did you know his real name, Mom?" I asked.

She winked at me. "Denny Diamond told me. Now let's get this show on the road."

"Right," Betty said. She and Reggie collected the picnic baskets and carried them outside. Ron followed them out. Jug waited with me as Mom locked up the house.

"Somehow," Jug confided, "I get the feeling that our tour troubles have just begun."

Chapter 7

Thanks to Gunny, we pulled into the deserted parking lot of the Rock Solid Dance Club in Hillside at around six o'clock. "We'll have to really hustle to get set up in time for the seven-thirty show," I said to Jug, beside me in the front seat. Jug nodded. I pulled the van up to a rear entrance of the building. In the side-view mirror I spotted Mom and the girls right behind us in the station wagon.

"Well, that was a fun four hours," Reggie groaned from the backseat. "Sitting here listening to Sleeping Beauty snore was a real hoot!" Reggie jerked a thumb toward the rear of the van, where Gunny was sprawled out, surrounded by luggage. He hadn't moved since we left Riverdale.

"Let's start setting up. Wake up Mr. Personality while I talk to my mother." I hopped out of the van just as Mom parked the wagon behind us. "How was the ride?" I asked. "Did I go too fast for you?"

"No, Archie," she replied. She and the girls got out of the car. "It's a good thing the traffic was light or we would never have made it here on time." I nodded. "I'll go inside and tell the owner we're here," Mom said. She turned and walked off toward the building's main entrance.

"How about we all help bring in the stuff," I proposed to Betty and Ron.

"Sure, Archie," Betty agreed.

Ron grimaced. "I'll help, but I'd better not break a nail." She held up her hand to inspect her perfect fingernails.

We reached the van just as Reg and Jug opened the back doors. Out stumbled a groggy Gunny. He shook his head, as if to clear his mind of cobwebs.

"Just point me in the direction of the stage," he said, climbing down. "I'm ready to play."

"First we have to set up," I replied. "Thanks to you, we probably won't even have enough time to warm up together."

"Don't sweat it, Archie," Gunny said. "I can wing it. I glanced through some of the arrangements you had in that crate in the back of the van before I nodded off." Gunny collected his guitar from the back of the van and slung it over his shoulder. "Well, I'm ready to go."

"You're not going anywhere," I ordered. "We need your help to unload."

Gunny shook his head. "Oh no," he refused. "I take care of my own stuff, and that's all."

Before I could say anything else, the back door of the building opened. Out came my mother with a chunky man dressed in a summer suit.

"This is Mr. Roberts, the owner of the Rock Solid Dance Club," Mom said, introducing us.

"How are you?" Mr. Roberts said. "I heard you had trouble getting started."

We all glanced at Gunny.

My mom quickly broke into the conversation. "I

explained to Mr. Roberts that we had an unexpected delay back in Riverdale."

"These things happen," Mr. Roberts sympathized. "If you need help with your stuff, I'll send out some of my staff to assist you."

"That would be great," I said. "Thanks."

"No problem," Mr. Roberts answered as he turned and headed back toward the club. "Just make sure you put on a good show tonight."

"Don't worry, sir," I called after him. "We will."

"Absolutely!" Gunny added.

"Are you folks ready to rock the house?" I called out to the audience at the Rock Solid later that evening. The crowd roared back. I glanced at Betty, Reg, and Ron. They smiled. I looked back at Jug. He twirled a drumstick. I shifted my eyes to my left. Gunny nodded and cranked up the volume dial of his electric guitar to the max.

"Then let's rock and roll!" I shouted. Ronnie kicked it off. The band started to play. Gunny followed right along, adding a few hot licks of his own whenever he could. I had to admit the guy was good. I took a deep breath and began to belt out the lyrics of our first song. By the end of the song, the crowd was sizzling. I looked over to my mom and Mr. Roberts, standing in the wings. Mom was smiling from ear to ear. She gave me a thumbs-up. Mr. Roberts nodded approvingly.

Gunny inched his way over to me. "I told you this would work out," he whispered, grinning. "Now let's rock the roof off of this joint." I nodded and grinned back.

"Do you want some more?" I yelled to the audience. The applause that answered my question was deafening. "Well, you've got it!" I cried as we went right into our next number.

That night The Archies carved out their own niche in local rock and roll history. I thought nothing could top winning that prize at the Teen Machine Dance Club, but I was wrong. There was magic in the air that night at the Rock Solid. The crowd wouldn't let us get offstage. We played every song we knew. And, like it or not, Gunny contributed a great deal to our success.

"That's all for tonight," I announced at last. "The show is over for now, but keep on rocking until we meet again." The lights dimmed and we slipped offstage as the crowd cheered, hooted, and clapped.

"You're the best band I've had here since Street Pack," Mr. Roberts told us as we stood backstage. "I'm just sorry I have you here for only one night."

"Maybe we'll be back again soon," I said.

"All you have to do is arrange it with Denny Diamond," my mother added. "Why don't you give him a call tomorrow?"

Mr. Roberts smiled. "I will," he responded before leaving us.

"We're a hit," Ron exclaimed. "Did you see all those cute boys giving us the eye while we were onstage?" She nudged Betty.

"My eyes were on one cute boy," Betty said. She winked at me.

"I can barely keep *my* eyes open," said Jug. "It's been a long day. I'm too tired to even eat."

Coming from Jughead, that was an amazing state-ment. Of course, considering that Jug had polished off most of the food in the picnic baskets and his lunch pail before the show, it was understandable.

"I'm sort of beat, myself," I admitted. The exhil-aration of performing was quickly being replaced by weariness. "Luckily our motel is just down the street."

"I think we could all use a good night's sleep," my mother said. She looked around. "If no one has any objections, I suggest we get our stuff back into the van and head right for the motel." Mom's expression suddenly changed. "Where are Reggie and Gunny?" she asked.

We all looked around. For the first time, we no-ticed they were gone. In all the excitement, we hadn't missed them. "Maybe they went outside for a breath of fresh air while the club empties out," I offered.

"Maybe," my mom said. "Let's find out." We walked to the rear door that led out to the parking lot. When we opened the door, we found Gunny and Reggie loading their gear into the van.

"We wondered where you guys had disappeared to," I said. I motioned toward the van. "Why are you so ambitious? We don't have to pack up that fast."

"I told you, I always take care of my own stuff," Gunny replied. He looked at Reg. "Besides, Reggie and I don't want to keep the ladies waiting, do we, Reg?"

"No way," Reggie answered. He pushed an am-plifier into the van.

"What ladies?" my mom asked.

"While you guys were talking to Mr. Roberts, Reggie and I went out onto the dance floor and met some girls who are having a party tonight," Gunny explained.

"And they invited us," Reggie said. "They're picking us up out front."

I glanced at my mom. She had a stern look on her face. "I'm sorry, but you're not going to any party, Reggie," my mom said. She looked at Gunny. "And I don't think you should, either."

Reggie's face froze. He looked like he was trying to speak, but no words came out.

"Whoa! Back off, Mary," Gunny said, raising his hands. "No one tells me where I can go." He motioned toward the rest of us. "You can be a nanny to the rest of these babies if you want to, but leave me alone." He finished putting his gear into the van.

"B-b-but Mrs. Andrews—" Reggie pleaded.

My mom shook her head. "It's out of the question, Reggie," she said. "Gunny is twenty-two years old and can take care of himself. You can't."

Just then a convertible pulled up a short distance away. Four girls waited inside. The driver honked the horn.

"That's my ride," said Gunny, moving toward the car. "It's too bad your baby-sitter won't let you have any real fun, Reg," Gunny called. "I'll tell you all about the party later, back at the motel." He climbed into the car with the girls. They sounded the horn one last time. Then they sped off.

"Cheer up, Reg," I said. "There'll be other parties." Reggie just shrugged and shook his head.

My mom put her arm around Reggie. "I'm sorry I had to do that, Reggie," she said. "If your mom were here she wouldn't have let you go, either."

"I know," Reggie moaned, "but what's the good of being a rock star if you can't have any fun?"

"Let's pack up," Jug suggested. "I'm bushed."

I peeked at my mom. She looked angry. I could tell she was mad at Gunny.

"I told you he'd be nothing but trouble," I whispered.

Mom smiled. "He's a pain in the neck, but he sure can play that guitar."

I smiled, too. "It's not easy to get ahead in the music business, is it?" I asked. "Sometimes you have to put up with the craziest stuff."

Chapter 8

At breakfast the next morning, we sat in the motel restaurant and watched Jughead pack away stack after stack of blueberry pancakes.

"Are you going for the world record or what?" I asked Jug after his fourth serving.

"Leave him alone and let him enjoy himself," my mom ordered. She took a sip of her coffee.

"Wouldn't it be nice if we could eat like that and never gain a pound?" Ron remarked to Betty.

"It sure would," Betty replied. Betty and Ron had had toast and cereal with skim milk for breakfast. Reg, Mom, and I had ordered scrambled eggs and ham. Gunny had yet to appear at the table.

"Did you wake Gunny for breakfast?" my mom asked Reggie. Reg and Gunny were sharing a room for the tour.

Reggie nodded. "I woke him up, but I'm not sure he's going to make it to the table. He didn't crawl into bed until after four in the morning."

I shook my head. It was now nine o'clock. We'd planned to leave for Southside Glen, the next stop on this leg of the tour, by ten. "If he's late again, I'll freak," I said.

A few minutes later Gunny appeared at the entrance to the restaurant. His long hair was a mess, and he looked like he'd slept in his clothes. He saw us and made his way toward our table.

"Morning, all," grunted Gunny when he reached the table. He pulled up a nearby chair and sat down. "We were great last night."

"You don't look so great," I replied.

Gunny looked at me through bleary eyes. "The life of a rock musician is never easy," he sighed. "Playing rock and partying all night can sure wear a guy down."

"Well, I would suggest you do less partying," my mom said.

Gunny didn't answer. He just shrugged as our waitress came up.

"Would you like some breakfast?" she asked Gunny.

"I'll just have coffee, black," he said.

"Oh no you won't," my mom corrected. She looked at the waitress. "Bring him some orange juice, a stack of pancakes, and some sausage," my mom ordered.

"But—" Gunny protested.

"No buts," my mom said. The waitress nodded and walked away.

"Why did you do that?" Gunny asked.

"Because you didn't eat a thing yesterday, and you're too skinny," my mom said. "I'm here to look after the members of this band, and that includes you. You can't rock and roll if you don't eat."

"That's for sure," Jug said, forking more sausage into his mouth.

Gunny slumped over the table.

"But I can't pay for that food," he grunted, embarrassed. "I'm broke until I get my share of the cash for these gigs."

I was kind of shocked to hear him admit that.

"Don't look at me like that," Gunny ordered. "Everyone knows young musicians are always broke. I used the last cash I had to pay my rent before we left."

"Food money comes out of the band's expense account," my mom said. "We'll figure out who owes what after we all get paid. Understand?"

"That's right," I agreed. "On this tour we share everything. When one eats, we all eat."

Betty smiled at Gunny. "And if you get hungry between meals, I have a big batch of homemade cookies in the station wagon. They're in a brown bag. Just help yourself."

Jug's ears perked right up. "Thanks," he said to Betty. "We will."

Gunny scratched his head in surprise. "I've been in lots of bands since I got out of high school." He shook his head. "It's always been every man for himself. I'm not sure I can get used to this one for all and all for one stuff."

The waitress brought Gunny's order. He began to eat.

"I'll pay the check and we'll start packing up," my mom said. She looked at Gunny. "Take your time eating. And there's plenty of time to shower and shave before you meet us in the parking lot."

We all started to get up. "Take your time, but be there at ten o'clock," I said, grinning at Gunny. He nodded as he forked pancakes into his mouth.

The rest of us left him at the table. "I guess we've got a lot to learn about this business," I said. "And the people in it."

Betty nodded. "I guess making it in the music business is harder than we thought."

"And much less glamorous," Ron added.

"If you have to be hungry to make it big," Jug said, "you can count me out." He looked at Betty. "Now where did you say you put those cookies?"

We managed to check out of the motel and hit the road right on time. Our schedule called for us to arrive in Southside Glen on Thursday afternoon. We were scheduled to rehearse at the Rock Quarry Dance Club on Thursday night and then play there on Friday and Saturday nights before heading back to Riverdale.

The ride from Hillside to Southside Glen was a long one. Once again the guys rode in the van and the girls followed in the wagon. At first I handled the driving while Reggie and Jug just relaxed. Gunny used the drive to catch up on his sleep. He didn't wake up until we stopped for a late lunch at a drive-through fast-food place. After our stop, Reg took over the driving so I could relax and eat my lunch.

"Hey, Gunny," I called as I munched on some french fries. "You don't have to spend the entire trip in isolation. Why don't you climb in the backseat with Jug and join us."

"Yeah," Reggie added. "You should be able to squeeze in next to that ton of food he has back there." Jug had placed a huge order at the fast-food joint— it seemed like he'd ordered everything on the menu.

"Okay," Gunny called, "but I'm really fine here. In fact, I was just looking through some of your old arrangements back here and found something I really like."

"Oh," I said, looking toward the back. I saw Gunny clamber out of the storage area and over the backseat. He had a hamburger in one hand and some sheets of music in the other. "Which arrangement?"

" 'Riverdale Rock,' " Gunny replied. He eased himself into the seat near Jug.

Reggie glanced at me. "Were you working on that again, Arch?" he asked.

"Yeah," I said. "I made a few changes last night at the motel. I couldn't sleep after the show. The song is better now, but it's still not ready to go."

"Yo!" Gunny said. "This thing has real potential. I think we should add it to the act for our shows at the Rock Quarry."

I shook my head. "It's not ready," I repeated.

"All it needs is a big guitar solo in the middle to make it work," Gunny said.

"No way," I said firmly. "A change like that would be great for the guitarist, but it would play down the contributions from the rest of the band."

Gunny leaned closer to the front seat. "I'm telling you, it would work," he insisted. "Let's give it a try. I'll work out the changes myself."

"Forget it," I ordered. "I've been working on that number a long time. It's something special I wrote, just for The Archies. It gives every member of the band a chance to shine. I'm not going to mess it up now just to please you."

Gunny dropped back against the seat so violently that he almost made Jug spill his milk shake.

"Hey! Watch it," Jug griped.

Gunny ignored him. "You just want to keep me from getting a solo," Gunny accused me.

"Listen, Gunny," I said. "It's *my* song. If I don't want to change it, I don't have to." I looked at him. "Now if you don't mind, put it back in the crate, where you found it."

Gunny glared at me. "Sure, Arch. And I'll put myself back there, too." He climbed back over the seat, into the rear of the van.

Reggie sneaked a peek in my direction. "What's the big deal, Arch?" he whispered. "Why don't you let him take a whack at your song?" Gunny seemed to be winning Reggie over to his side.

"Because it's *my* song, Reg," I said. "Now quit bugging me about it and drive. We're almost there."

"Okay, Arch," said Reggie, "but things were just starting to smooth out between you and Gunny. Did you have to make waves again?"

I stared at Reggie. "It's my song," I muttered. "And I'm not the person who's causing a problem."

No one had much to say the rest of the way to Southside Glen. We arrived at the Rock Quarry Dance Club around three in the afternoon. The owner, Ted Cobb, was waiting for us. He was a tall, thin man with long but neatly groomed gray hair. "Welcome to the Rock Quarry," he said as we unloaded our stuff. "I'm sure you'll enjoy working here. Denny Diamond speaks highly of your group."

"Thank you," my mother replied, following Mr. Cobb into the building.

As I watched my mother and Mr. Cobb walk away, Betty and Ronnie came up to me. "What's bugging Gunny?" Betty asked me.

I shrugged. "He's mad because I won't let him rework 'Riverdale Rock' so he can do a big solo."

It was Betty's turn to shrug. "But we don't even do 'Riverdale Rock' in our show," she said.

"I know," I replied, "but he wants us to. He found the number in the back of the van during our drive over here."

"Too bad for him," Betty said. "It's your song, Archie." She looked at Ronnie. "Right, Ron?"

"I guess," Ronnie replied, and shrugged. I wondered if Ronnie, like Reggie, was becoming a Gunny Witherspoon supporter.

"Let's forget about it for now and start rehearsal," I suggested.

"Let's," Betty agreed. We picked up our stuff and headed for the building Jug and Reggie had just entered.

Rehearsal went well despite Gunny's barely speaking to me. When we were finished, Mr. Cobb clapped loudly. "Great!" he said. "The Archies are everything Denny said they were. I'm looking forward to tomorrow night's show."

"So are we, Mr. Cobb," I said. We started to collect our stuff.

"Well, gang," said Mom. "What would you like to do tonight? I see no reason why we should have to stay locked in our motel rooms after dinner." She smiled. "Mr. Cobb said there's a movie theater just down the street from the motel. How about if we all take in a flick? It's my treat."

"That sounds great," said Betty. She moved close to me and slipped her hand into mine. "Doesn't it, Archie?"

"It does," I agreed.

"Why not?" said Reggie. He looked at Gunny. "I'm agreeable, unless my roommate can arrange something better—like a party."

"No parties and no movie for me tonight," Gunny said. "I'm staying in my room. I've got work to do."

"Work?" asked Jughead, baffled. "What kind of work?"

"You'll find out tomorrow," Gunny answered. He picked up his guitar and walked off.

"What's with him?" my mom asked in puzzlement.

"I don't know, but I wish he were going to the movies with us," Ron said. It sounded to me like she was developing one of her famous short-term crushes. I liked Ron, and she liked me, but she became infatuated with the strangest guys sometimes.

"Gunny sure is an odd young man," my mom said. "But let's not let him spoil our fun." She looked at Reggie. "Who knows? We might even meet some young ladies at the theater."

Reggie perked right up. "I never thought of that," he exclaimed. "If we do, I could invite them to our show tomorrow night to see us rock the house."

Chapter 9

The next day Gunny didn't have much to say at breakfast or lunch. He kept silent while the rest of us chatted about the gory horror flick we'd seen the night before. I sensed that something was up with Gunny, but I didn't know what. Later that afternoon, as we were preparing to leave for the Rock Quarry, I learned what was on Gunny's mind. Jug and I were packing stuff into the van when Gunny and Reg came walking up with their guitars. In his hand, Gunny had some sheets of music.

"I want to talk to you, Arch," Gunny said.

"What about?" I asked.

"This." Gunny practically shoved the papers into my face.

I glanced at the music on the paper and recognized the song immediately. It was a copy of "Riverdale Rock," with some major revisions.

"I told you to leave this song alone," I said to Gunny.

"Don't brush me off just like that," Gunny said. "I worked all night and half the day on those revisions." He jabbed a finger in the direction of the sheet music. "Check it out. It's good. In fact, it's great." Gunny looked at Reggie. "Tell him, Reg!"

Reggie nodded. "It is, Arch," he agreed. "Gunny and I were just playing it up in our room. It's hot."

"What's hot?" Ronnie said as she, Betty, and my mom walked up to us.

"Gunny's version of 'Riverdale Rock,'" explained Reggie.

Betty looked at me. "I thought you were going to leave that song alone until you had time to polish it up."

"I did the polishing for him," Gunny said. "That song is perfect now. We should be doing it in our show." Gunny smiled. "Why don't we add it to tonight's program? How about it, Reg? Ron? What do you think?"

"Yeah, sure!" agreed Reggie.

"It makes no difference to me," Ronnie said.

"It makes a difference to me!" Betty fired back. "We've been waiting a long time to do that number."

"It's Archie's decision, because it's Archie's song," said Jug. "Revisions or not, it still belongs to Archie."

My mom just listened to the conversation without saying anything.

"I know it's Archie's song," Gunny admitted, "but if my revisions make the song good for the group, why shouldn't we do it?" He smirked. "We *are* a group, aren't we?"

I nodded. "I'll look the song over on the way to the club," I agreed—but not too enthusiastically. "If I feel it's good for all of us, I'll consider doing it at tomorrow's show." I tucked the papers under my arm. "And if I think it's more of a one-man show than a group piece, we won't do it." I looked at Gunny.

Gunny shrugged. "Whatever you think, man," he said. "This is your band. I'm just the lead guitarist." Gunny walked off toward the van.

"I think I'll ride in the wagon today," I said.

"Good," Ron said. "I'll go in the van with the rest of the boys." She smiled and turned to walk away.

"I'll drive the van, Arch," Jug offered. Jug, Reg, Ron, and Gunny got into the van.

I followed Betty and Mom over to the wagon. I sat in the backseat alone. As we drove off, I studied the revised song.

"Well?" asked Betty. "How is it?"

"It's good," I admitted, "but it's not an Archies tune now. It's nothing but a showcase for Gunny's guitar playing, with tiny bits for the rest of us. He's even cut out some of the lyrics I worked so hard on." I handed the music to Betty. "Here!" I said. "See what you think."

Betty took the papers and looked them over.

"Is Archie right, or is he exaggerating?" my mom wanted to know.

Betty shook her head. "This is nothing like the original 'Riverdale Rock,' " Betty agreed. "The original gave each member of the band a chance to shine with solos. This new version highlights Gunny on lead guitar, and that's all."

"Well then, drop this version," Mom said. "I mean, drop it if you want to," she quickly clarified. "It seems to me that Gunny would like to use The Archies as a stepping-stone to his own success rather than help promote the band as a whole."

"It's too bad Reggie and Ronnie don't see it that way," I commented.

"They're just infatuated with Gunny's rock-musician life-style,"Betty said."But they won't be fooled for long. Soon they'll see this song issue for what it really is."

"I hope so," I said as we approached the club, "because there's no way I'm going to agree to do 'Riverdale Rock' the way it is."

We pulled into the club's lot and parked near the rear entrance. As soon as we got out of the car, Gunny came over to me. "Well?" he asked. "How about it? Are we adding 'Riverdale Rock' to the act or not?"

"It's good, Gunny," I said, "but it's not an Archies number. I don't see how we can do it. I'm sorry."

Gunny stared at me. "Not as sorry as you're going to be," he grumbled. "I'm not going to let a chance like this pass me by." He turned and walked off in a huff.

"Phew! He sure was steamed," Betty said.

"We can't worry about that now," I answered. "We've got a show to do." I put the sheets of music in the van.

Gunny stayed mad up until show time. As the Rock Quarry filled with people, Gunny's mood seemed to lighten a bit. As egotistical and opportunistic as he was, he was also a quality performer.

"Are you ready?" I asked him as Mr. Cobb went out to introduce us.

"Gunny Witherspoon is always ready," he answered. "In the hostile jungle of rock, I'm a survivor, dude."

"And here they are—after a smash engagement in Hillside," announced Mr. Cobb. "The Archies!"

We dashed onstage, where our instruments were waiting for us. The crowd cheered and shouted.

"It's time to shake it down and rock this town!" I yelled to the audience. "Let's get it done, Archies!" The band began to play. Our first number knocked the crowd out, just as it had in Hillside. The room was buzzing as we rolled right into our next song. At the halfway point of our show, the place was rocking to the rafters.

"We might never get out of here alive," Reggie whispered to me as we got ready to finish up our act. "This audience loves us."

I nodded to Reg and looked back at the crowd. I held the hand mike close to my mouth. "Here we go one more time!" I shouted. We went into our final number. When we finished, the kids still wanted more. I glanced toward the wings, where Mr. Cobb and my mom were standing. Nothing like this had ever happened to us before. I wasn't exactly sure what to do.

"Give them another number," Mr. Cobb called out to me.

"Without missing a beat, Gunny picked up a mike. "So you want more?" he yelled. "Okay! Here's something brand-new we've been working on. It's called 'Riverdale Rock!'"

The crowd hooted and hollered. I looked at Gunny smirking as he began to kick off the intro. I had been caught completely off guard by his actions. There was no choice but to follow. The band picked up the beat, and Gunny cranked out one of the greatest guitar solos I'd ever heard. It was awesome. When we finished the number, the audience cheered wildly.

"That's it! Until tomorrow night, we're out of here," I announced. We all dashed off the stage into the wings.

The minute we were out of the audience's sight, I confronted Gunny. "What's the big idea, you jerk!" I said. "Don't ever pull anything like that again, or else."

"Or else what?" he sneered. "What are you going to do, kick me out of the band? We need each other, remember? This is the way Denny wants it." He smirked. "No Gunny, no deal." His comment left me speechless.

"Chill out, Arch," said Reg. "The number went over great. Everyone loved it."

"They loved Gunny," Ron gushed.

"Yeah," said Jug. "Before you know it, we'll be calling ourselves The Gunnies!"

At that moment my mother and Mr. Cobb came over. "Great show," Mr. Cobb complimented. "And that last number was terrific. I want you to use it as the closing number again tomorrow. It's a real killer." He looked at me. "Okay?"

"No problem," Gunny said, answering for me. "Right, Arch?"

I shook my head. "Nope. No problem."

My mom looked at me as Gunny walked off with Mr. Cobb at his side and Reggie and Ronnie in tow.

"I think there is a problem," she whispered. "And I'm not sure how to solve it."

Our second show at the Rock Quarry was an even bigger smash than opening night. The crowd loved "Riverdale Rock" even though I still felt it didn't belong in the act.

Mr. Cobb was so happy with the job we did that he personally helped us pack our stuff after the club closed. "Have a safe trip back to Riverdale," he called as we prepared to get into our vehicles. He closed the door from inside the club, and we heard the lock click shut.

"It'll be good to get home," Jug said as we stood near the van. "I miss my mom's home cooking."

"I miss sleeping in my own bed," said Betty.

"I miss my wardrobe," Ron added. "On our next trip, I'm going to have to bring more luggage."

"We've got a lot of rehearsing to do before we go back on the road," I said. "I expect to see you all at my house on Monday afternoon."

"Oh no," groaned Reggie. "It's back to that smelly old garage."

"Garage?" asked Gunny.

"It's where we rehearse," I explained.

"Is that a fact?" Gunny remarked snidely.

I'd just about had it with Mr. Gunther Witherspoon. I hadn't made a big deal about the dirty stunt he'd pulled performing "Riverdale Rock" onstage the night before. I figured it wouldn't do any good to divide the band over it, so I had let the issue drop. But I wasn't about to take anything else from him.

"I suggest you all be there if you want to get your share of the money for this half of the tour," my mom quickly broke in. She knew me well enough to know that my patience with Gunny was just about at an end. "Denny will be bringing me the money to pay out," she continued. "So, no show, no dough."

"I'll be there, and right on time," Reggie said, smiling from ear to ear.

"So will I," seconded Gunny. "Money talks to me very loudly."

"Good," I said. "Now let's quit wasting time standing around an empty parking lot and head for home." We got into our vehicles and sped off into the night.

Chapter 10

I was in my room, working on *my* version of "Riverdale Rock," when my mother knocked on the door.

"Archie, Denny Diamond is downstairs," she announced.

"I guess I was so busy I didn't hear the doorbell ring," I said. I followed my mother down to the living room, where Denny was waiting.

Denny got up from the sofa as soon as he saw me. "Archie," he said, smiling. "I've been hearing great things about your first few club dates." We shook hands, and then we all sat down.

"They went pretty well," I admitted.

"*Pretty* well?" Denny chuckled. "Ted Cobb and Jack Roberts raved about the job you did. I can book you at their clubs anytime."

"The two of them were very nice and helpful," my mom said. She stood up. "Would you care for something to drink, Denny?"

"No thanks," he said.

"Well, how about staying for lunch?" Mom invited. "The band is rehearsing here this afternoon. You could say hello to them."

"I'd like to," said Denny, "but I'm really pressed

73

for time." He looked in my direction. "Jimmy Street is in Martinsville this week, visiting his folks, and I have to run over there. It's a sort of combination business/pleasure meeting."

"That sounds interesting," I replied.

Denny nodded. "Jimmy is about to launch his own record label. It's not a big secret, but it's not known by a lot of people yet, either. He's scouting the country, looking for new talent to sign. I may be working with him."

"Congratulations," my mom said.

I leaned over the coffee table that separated Denny and me. "What will that mean to our deal?" I asked.

"Basically nothing now," Denny said, "but it could mean more down the road. I'm going to try to get Jimmy to see your show in Martinsville. If he likes you, The Archies could be on their way to a recording contract." Denny leaned back on the sofa. "Of course, even if he likes your sound he might think you're a year or two away from being ready to record."

My mom studied Denny. "What do you think?" she asked.

"I think The Archies are close to being ready, but I don't own a record company," Denny admitted. "By the way, how are things working out with Gunny as your lead guitarist?"

I slumped in my chair. "The truth is," I answered, "Gunny is a great guitarist, but he's also a trouble-maker. He and I just don't see eye to eye."

Denny looked at my mom for elaboration. "Gunny is a little self-centered," my mom explained. "And the fact that he's older than the other members of the band causes some conflicts."

Denny shook his head. "I was hoping that adding him to The Archies would be the finishing touch for your band." Denny stood up. "I'll have a talk with him the first chance I get. Maybe you two can iron out your differences during the second leg of the tour."

"I sure hope so," I said. Frankly, though, I had my doubts.

"I think the band will be glad to get this," Denny said. He reached into the inside pocket of his coat and took out an envelope, which he handed to my mother. "Here are the checks for the first three shows. The band's cut was fifteen hundred dollars. That means each band member gets two hundred and fifty bucks."

"I'll see that they get it," Mom assured Denny.

Denny looked at his watch. "Well, that's all for now. I've got to run."

Mom and I walked Denny to the front door.

"You have the details and schedule for this week's appearances," Denny said. "Phone me on Wednesday if you have any questions before you go on the road again." Then he added, "I may see you in Martins-ville. Try to make that show something special. If I can swing it, Jimmy Street will be in the audience to give you the once-over."

I nodded. "Should I tell the rest of the band about that?"

Denny shook his head. "I think it would be better if you kept it under your hat for now. It's not a definite thing, and I believe young bands play better when there is no pressure on them."

"Okay," I agreed, "but I don't like keeping news like that from my friends."

"It's for the best," Denny assured me. "Trust me, I know what I'm saying."

I nodded. "You're our manager."

Denny chuckled. "And don't you forget it," he said. "Bye, Mary. Bye, Archie." He walked off toward his car.

I shut the front door. "Well," said my mom, "things sure seem to be happening very quickly."

"Maybe too quickly," I remarked. I started back upstairs.

"Where are you going?" Mom asked. "The band will be here for rehearsal in a little while."

"I know," I replied. "But I've almost got 'Riverdale Rock' worked out. With a little luck, I can finish it before rehearsal today."

"What about Gunny's version?" Mom wanted to know.

"His version will be dropped," I said. "We'll substitute the original at the end of our show in its place."

"Gunny won't like that," my mother warned me.

I stopped midstep. " 'Riverdale Rock' was written for The Archies," I stated. "Gunny has a small part in my version, same as everyone else. If he wants to be a member of The Archies, he'd better like it."

"I'll give a shout when the band shows up," my mom called as I headed for my room. "Meanwhile, I'll make snacks for everyone."

Time flew by as I labored over the notes of "Riverdale Rock." I'd just put my pencil down for good when I heard my mom call me. "Archie! Reggie, Betty, and Jughead are here."

"I'll be right there," I called back. I picked up the sheets of music and stared at them. "*Now* the song is perfect," I said to myself. Music in hand, I trudged downstairs. Reg, Betty, and Jug were waiting for me in the living room.

"Hi, Archie," Betty greeted me. She noticed the papers in my hand. "What's that?"

" 'Riverdale Rock,' " I announced proudly, holding up the sheet music. "It's finally the way I want it." I handed it to Betty.

"But we're already doing 'Riverdale Rock,' " Reggie protested.

"This is the way we're going to be doing it from now on," I said.

"It's awesome," Betty complimented. She handed me back the music. "I can't wait to play it."

"Why wait?" I suggested. "Let's go out to the garage and kick it around until Ron and Gunny get here."

"Super!" Betty exclaimed. She got up.

"Shouldn't we wait for Ron and Gunny?" Reggie asked as he, too, got up.

"Yeah. Let's wait in the kitchen," proposed Jug. "I'm kind of hungry."

"No way," I said firmly. "We'll eat after rehearsal." I eyed Jug. "In fact, my mom is busy out in the kitchen right now making sandwiches for us."

Jug smiled. "Maybe we can help her," he suggested.

"She doesn't need any help," I said. "But *we* need to rehearse."

We made our way to the garage, where our instruments were already set up. We'd unpacked the van on Sunday when we'd arrived home.

"If this song sounds as good as it looks, it could become a big hit," Betty remarked as she switched on the keyboard.

"Right," kidded Jug, sitting down behind his drums. "Maybe it'll be our first gold record."

"I still think we should wait for Ron and Gunny," Reg said. He opened his case and took out his bass.

"Let's just run through it a few times," I said, strapping on my guitar. I counted off, and we began to play and sing, following the music I'd handed out. The song sounded just as great as I'd hoped it would. We were still playing when Gunny and Ronnie walked into the garage together.

We stopped as soon as we saw them. "How about that?" Ron grumbled. "They started rehearsal without us." She looked at Gunny. "You were right, Gunny," she continued. "The band doesn't appreciate me enough."

"Huh?" I sputtered. "What are you talking about, Ron?"

"When we were walking up to the house, Gunny told me I should have more solos," Ronnie stated. "He said my singing talent is being ignored."

I glared at Gunny. "You have a small solo in 'Riverdale Rock,' " I told Ron.

Ron looked surprised. "I do?"

"Sure," I answered. I showed her the song we'd been playing and pointed out her part.

"Oh, Archiekins," she purred. "Thank you." She threw her arms around me and kissed me on the cheek.

"I'd kiss you, too, if I thought it would help land me a good solo," Gunny said.

"You have a small solo, too," I replied. "We all do."

Gunny nodded. "So I heard," he grumbled, "but I like my arrangement of 'Riverdale Rock' better."

"That figures," said Jug.

"I guess this means my version is out," Gunny said.

I shook my head. "Not out," I reassured him. "We'll just put it on the shelf, except for special occasions."

Gunny scowled. "Maybe I should be put on the shelf, too—except for special occasions?" he remarked acidly.

"Denny wouldn't like that," I answered. "He wants you to fit in with The Archies—and so do I."

"I see," said Gunny. "You want me to fit in . . . like a round peg in a square hole."

"Suit yourself," I said. I turned away from him. "Now, can we start rehearsing?" I handed Gunny a copy of "Riverdale Rock." "We'll lead off with this."

"Maybe I'll just take off instead," Gunny said. "Rehearsal is for wimps, anyway."

Just then my mom entered the garage.

"It's payday," she announced, holding up Denny's envelope. She smiled and began to hand out the checks.

"Don't let this be severance pay," I told Gunny. "The band needs you."

Gunny put down his guitar case and opened his check, then put it in his pocket. "I already told you money talks to me," Gunny said to me. "And this check just told me to stay."

I nodded. "Now that everyone has been paid for our first three shows, let's get ready for the next three," I urged.

Ronnie studied her check disappointedly. "Two hundred and fifty dollars? Is that all we get? My allowance is more than that."

We all glared at her.

She gulped and stuffed the check in her jeans pocket. She walked over to her keyboard. "Okay! Okay!" she announced. "I'm ready. Let's play 'Riverdale Rock.' "

Chapter 11

That Thursday we hit the road again. We were scheduled to start the second half of our mini-tour in Edgewater, in a club called the Music Mansion. This time we left Riverdale promptly at ten o'clock in the morning, as planned. Gunny actually seemed to be looking forward to playing in Edgewater.

"The Music Mansion is a good club," Gunny said as we headed the convoy in our van.

Reggie, who was driving, glanced at Gunny, in the backseat with Jug.

"How do you know that?" Reggie asked.

"I played there when I was in a group called Busted Luck," Gunny explained. "We were the house band at the Mansion for a little while."

"What happened to Busted Luck?" I asked.

"It broke up—like most of the other bands I've played with," Gunny said, shrugging. "It was too bad. We could have gone somewhere, if the leader of the band hadn't decided to go solo."

"What do you mean?" inquired Jug.

"Our lead singer's name was Tony Malone," Gunny answered. "He was a good singer and a fair song-writer. A small record company offered him a chance to record on his own, so he just split and that was the end of the band."

"Did Tony ever make it big?" Reggie asked.

"Nah," said Gunny. "After a few flops, the record company ripped up his contract. Now he's working nine to five, like most of the other guys from that group. I think I'm the only member of Busted Luck who's still playing full-time."

"Gee, that's tough," Reggie said.

"Maybe it is, and maybe it isn't," Gunny said. "Wild Willie Williams, the drummer, saved enough bread to buy himself a music store in Edgewater. I hear he's doing real well."

"Now I understand why you're so eager to play in Edgewater," I said to Gunny. "Is your friend coming to our show?"

"Are you kidding?" said Gunny. "Wild Willie is going to be waiting for me in the parking lot when we arrive." Gunny laughed. "When I phoned and told him I was playing Edgewater with a new group, he insisted on meeting me at the club the minute we show up. He wants to take me out for lunch and give me a tour of his store."

"It's a good thing we left Riverdale early," I said. "That will give you and your buddy time to reminisce before the show."

Gunny leaned forward to look at me. "I'd have more time if I could skip the pre-show sound check," he said. "How about it, Arch? I don't really need any warm-up."

Jughead and Reg glanced at me. "Sure! Why not?" I answered. "Once we reach the club, take right off if you want to. There's no sense in your hanging around. Just be back in time for the seven o'clock show."

Gunny smiled and leaned back. "No sweat, man," he said. "Thanks, Arch. I appreciate it."

"No problem," I answered.

"Hey, Gunny," said Jug. "You played with Busted Luck and Snake Bite, and now you're with The Archies. How many bands have you been in, anyway?"

"Too many," Gunny said, glancing out the window at a sign that read Welcome to Edgewater. He sighed. "I guess I've been in about a dozen or so bands since I started playing in high school."

Jug shook his head. "The only band I've ever been in is The Archies."

"I hope it stays that way," I said.

We moved down the main street of Edgewater. It was a town about twice the size of Riverdale. The directions Denny had printed up for us made it easy to find the Music Mansion. We pulled into the club's parking lot at about one-thirty. As usual we parked near a rear door and got out to unload our stuff. Since we weren't in any rush, Betty and Ron went into the club with my mom to speak to the manager there.

While Jug, Reg, Gunny, and I were waiting to unpack the van, a small red pickup truck came zooming into the lot. The truck sped over to where we were standing and screeched to a stop. Out jumped a tall, thin guy with shoulder-length blond hair pulled back in a ponytail.

"Yo! Gunny, my man!" yelled the driver of the truck, racing up to us. "What's up, dude?"

"Wild Willie! Hey!" Gunny shouted back. They hugged each other and then slapped hands repeatedly.

"How's the music-store business, man?" asked Gunny.

"Okay! It's okay!" Willie replied. He glanced at us. "So you're on the road with a new group. What happened to Snake Bite?"

Gunny shrugged. "They were going nowhere, man. My new band is about to skyrocket. The Archies are going places, Willie. Just wait until you check us out tonight."

"The Archies," Willie said. "A dude who was in my store the other day mentioned The Archies." Willie moved closer. "I heard you rocked the walls at the Rock Quarry last week."

Reggie grinned. "Yup! That was us," he said. Gunny introduced us to Wild Willie. Willie was especially friendly to Jug, perhaps because they were both drummers.

"So is it okay if we split to talk over old times?" Willie asked Gunny.

"Sure. Let's do it," Gunny answered.

"Solid, man." Willie slapped Gunny's hand, and the two of them hopped in Willie's truck. Willie sounded the horn and away they sped. At that moment the back door of the Music Mansion opened and out walked Betty and Ron. They watched the truck peel out of the parking lot.

"Who was that?" Ron asked.

"Gunny and a friend of his named Wild Willie Williams," I answered.

84

"Gunny?" said Betty. "But what about the sound check?"

"It's okay," I told her. "I'll explain later."

"Did I hear you say the name Gunny?"

I looked back over my shoulder and saw a husky bald-headed man standing next to my mother.

"This is Mr. Rivers," my mother said. "He's the manager of the Music Mansion."

"You're not talking about Gunny Witherspoon, are you?" Mr. Rivers asked.

I nodded. "Yes. He's our lead guitarist," I replied.

Mr. Rivers raised his eyebrows.

"Do you know him?" I inquired.

It was Mr. Rivers's turn to nod. "He played here with that crazy friend of his, Willie Williams, years ago when I first took over the club."

"That's right," Reggie said. "Their band was called Busted Luck. Were they any good?"

"They were good, but unreliable—especially Willie," Mr. Rivers answered.

"Well, don't worry about The Archies," I told Mr. Rivers. "We're totally reliable. We always start our shows on time."

Betty and I looked at each other as we waited backstage at the Music Mansion. The audience was getting restless. The show was supposed to have started fifteen minutes earlier. "What are we going to do?" Betty asked.

"What we're going to do," said my mother, answering for me, "is to go on without Gunny."

Reggie came rushing up to where we were standing. He'd been at the back door, hoping Gunny would arrive in time for the show. We hadn't seen him since he'd left with his friend that afternoon.

"He's not going to make it, Arch," Reggie said.

"We can't stall any longer, Arch," Jughead added. "Mr. Rivers is starting to look a little hot under the collar, and the crowd is getting rowdy." Sure enough, the audience had begun to clap to get the show started.

"I'll play lead guitar," I decided out loud. I strapped on my instrument and signaled across the stage to Mr. Rivers. Mr. Rivers walked out onstage from the opposite wing. The angry crowd started to boo and jeer.

"They're in an ugly mood now," Reggie said, peeking out at the packed house.

"In that case, let's open with the new 'Riverdale Rock,' " I said. "That will get them in a better mood."

"Here they are," Mr. Rivers announced. "Take it away, Archies!"

"Good luck," my mom called as we raced onstage. The audience's reception was less than enthusiastic.

"I know the show didn't start on time," I said, "but now the time is ripe for some good old-fashioned rock and roll. So let's go!" I turned to the band. We began to jam. The crowd's anger melted away quickly, and soon the ocean of people in front of us was swaying and moving in time to the music. The song was an instant hit. The crowd really got into the new arrangement.

"Riverdale rock! Rock! Rock!" I sang, finishing the opening number.

"Riverdale rock! Rock! Rock!" Betty and Ron repeated as Reggie wound down the tune on his bass guitar.

When Jug hit the final beat, the crowd exploded in a wild display of appreciation. We had won them over with "Riverdale Rock." Even Mr. Rivers, who had looked furious when we first went on, was now smiling and clapping from the wings.

"How about some more?" I called to the crowd. They roared. We began our next number. As we did, Gunny came dashing out of the wings, his guitar already strapped on. With a quick glance in my direction, he shrugged and then plugged in his instrument. He quickly joined in without missing a beat.

The rest of the show went even better. After that opening number, the crowd was in our pocket. They loved everything we did. We got a thunderous ovation as we finished the show and raced offstage.

"Where were you?" I snapped at Gunny as soon as we were in the wings.

"It wasn't my fault, man," said Gunny. "Willie and I got hung up."

"As far as I'm concerned," said Betty, "it really didn't matter if you showed up or not. We were doing fine without you."

Gunny glared at Betty. "Without me around, The Archies are nothing," Gunny said.

"Sure," said Jughead. "And *with* you around, we have nothing but trouble."

"Hey!" said Gunny as the crowd in the club continued to roar. "Welcome to the strange world of rock and roll, pal. Sometimes things get a little hectic."

"That's enough bickering," my mother said. She

looked at Gunny. "It's up to Denny to decide what to do about incidents like this."

Gunny glared at my mom. "What are you going to do, Mary?" he said nastily. "Complain about me some more? Denny gave me a little lecture before we left this time. Don't worry, I promised him I'd be a good boy for my nanny on this trip." He turned and headed for the club's exit.

I was steamed. No one could speak to my mother like that. I started to go after Gunny, but Mom grabbed my arm and stopped me.

"Don't, Archie," she said. "It won't do any good. We've got to pack up and hit the road for Oak Knoll."

"But Mom—"

"Do you want me to say something to Gunny, Arch?" Reggie asked.

"He shouldn't have talked to you that way, Mrs. Andrews," Ronnie said.

Even Reggie and Ronnie were upset by Gunny's outburst.

"Don't do anything, Reggie," my mom insisted. "We'll just let this drop. It's a long drive to Oak Knoll for tomorrow's show. Maybe things will cool down by then."

I nodded. "They'd better," I said, "because if he ever talks to you like that again, there'll be no stopping me!"

Chapter 12

We left Edgewater very late and had to drive all night to reach Oak Knoll. The trip wasn't much fun. Each of us took a turn driving while the others slept. The only one who didn't drive—he didn't offer, and we didn't ask—was Gunny. He spent the entire trip curled up in the back of the van, snoring like an exhausted lumberjack.

I was behind the wheel of the van at nine o'clock the following morning when we approached the outskirts of Oak Knoll. We were booked to play an upscale place there called the Rockin' Horse. The Rockin' Horse had dressing rooms where we could shower and freshen up, so we'd decided not to check into our motel until later that night. We'd sleep over in Oak Knoll after our show at the Rockin' Horse and then leave for Martinsville the next morning.

As we moved down the highway, I saw a sign advertising a diner just ahead. Since we had time to spare, I thought it would be a good opportunity to stop for breakfast. I rolled down the window. As we approached the diner, I honked my horn and reached out the window with my arm to signal Betty, who was driving the station wagon behind me, to follow.

I turned into the diner's parking lot, and Betty followed me in.

"Wha-what's going on?" Reg sputtered as he sat up in the front seat. The horn had awakened him.

"I thought we'd stop here for breakfast," I answered.

"Breakfast!" enthused Jug. He snapped into a sitting position in the backseat. I laughed. The honking of the horn hadn't awakened him, but the mere mention of breakfast had instantly ended his deep sleep.

I pulled the van into a parking spot and turned off the motor. "We'll eat before we drive into town." I looked behind Jug. "You'd better wake up Sleeping Beauty back there," I said, pointing to Gunny. I opened the door and got out of the van.

Betty had parked the station wagon right next to us. She got out as I walked over to the car. "I'm glad you stopped," she said. "I'm starving."

My mom and Ron got out of the wagon. My mom yawned.

"This is the pits," Ron grumbled as she checked her looks in her compact mirror. "Yuck!" she shrieked. "I look terrible!"

"I think you look beautiful, Ron," I chuckled.

Ron snapped her compact shut. "Sure. Look at me!" she grumbled. "My hair is a mess. My blouse is all wrinkled." She gritted her teeth. "If I knew going on the road meant ending up like this, I would have stayed home." She shook her head. "I can't believe I actually slept in a car. Now I know what TV stars mean when they talk about the high cost of success."

"She's been grumbling like that every waking moment of this drive," Betty whispered to me.

My mom put her arm around Ron as Reggie and Jughead walked up to us. "I know how you feel, Ron," she said. "Sleeping in a car isn't much fun at my age, either. We'll both feel better after we freshen up and have a good meal."

Ron sighed. "I hope so," she said, "but I sincerely doubt it." Ron went back in the wagon and removed her makeup case from the back of the car. We all started for the diner's entrance.

"Where's Gunny?" I asked Jug. "Didn't you wake him?"

Jug nodded. "I woke him."

"Isn't he coming to breakfast?"

"He said he'd get there in his own good time," Reg said, shrugging. "Apparently the long drive didn't do much to cool his temper."

"If anyone should be mad, it's us," Betty said as we entered the diner. "If he wants to stew in the van, let him."

I was kind of surprised at Betty. Usually she was a live-and-let-live kind of person. Gunny had gotten on the wrong side of her the night they'd met at the Teen Machine Dance Club, and he'd stayed there ever since.

A hostess came up to us. "Six?" she asked.

"No, seven," my mom corrected. "Someone else will be joining us."

The hostess nodded and led us to a table. We sat down. Mom, Ron, and Betty went off to the ladies' room.

"I think I'm going to have a stack of pancakes and some sausage," Reggie said.

"I feel like ham and eggs," I said.

"That's what I want, too," Jug chimed in.

Reggie and I looked at him. "Which one?" I asked. "Ham and eggs, or pancakes and sausage?"

Jug licked his lips. "Both," he said, "and some hash brown potatoes, toast, juice, and maybe a bowl of cornflakes."

I turned toward the entrance and saw Gunny walk in. He spoke to the hostess and she led him to a single table on the other side of the room. Jug and Reggie watched as Gunny sat down by himself.

"What's that all about?" Jughead asked.

I shrugged. "You've got me."

"Maybe he didn't see us over here," Reggie said. Reg started to get up.

"He saw us," I said, pushing Reggie back down in his seat. "I think it's obvious that he doesn't want to sit with us." Gunny glanced in our direction and then turned away.

Betty, Ron, and my mother returned to the table and sat down. They all looked much better. Their hair was neat and they had washed their faces. "Didn't Gunny come in yet?" Mom asked.

"He came in," Jughead said. He pointed across the room to where Gunny was sitting.

"What's the problem?" Betty asked sarcastically.

"Who knows?" said Jughead. "And who cares?" he added.

"I'll go over and talk to him," my mom suggested.

I looked at her and shook my head. "I don't think

that's a good idea, Mom. We've all tried to make him feel like he's a part of The Archies, but Gunny insists on doing things his way. He plays with our group, but he's not really a member of our band." I put my elbows on the table. "This just isn't working out. After we finish these last two club dates I'll have to have a serious talk with Denny." I shook my head. "I don't think Gunny should remain a member of The Archies. We really don't need him, and it's an uncomfortable alliance at best. What do the rest of you guys think?" I looked around the table.

"I think he should leave the group," said Betty.

I looked at Ron. She hesitated. "He goes," she said. Reggie nodded.

I looked at Jug. "What do you think?"

"I think we should order," said Jug. "Here comes our waitress."

The waitress took our orders. The service was prompt and the food was good. The hearty breakfast made us feel a lot better. During the meal we talked about the show we had planned for the Rockin' Horse. We didn't bother to discuss Gunny again. In fact, we didn't even look over to where he was eating all alone.

"I think we should open with the new 'Riverdale Rock,' " Reggie said. "It wins the audience over to our side at the start."

"I think we should close with it," Betty disagreed. "Always save your best shot for last."

"I think Reggie is right," I agreed. "We should open with 'Riverdale Rock.' "

The waitress gave us our check and we all got up

to leave. It was then that we noticed Gunny had already gone outside.

"No matter what you plan to do about Gunny later," my mom advised, "I think you should try to end this feud right now. You still have two more shows to do together on this tour."

"I don't know, Mom," I said as we exited the diner. "He's not the easiest guy to get along with."

Mom looked at me. "Maybe that's because he's never been in a band where all the members are good friends who really care about each other."

"I think your mom's right, Arch," said Jug. "The Archies are kind of unique in that respect."

I looked over at where our vehicles were parked. Gunny was leaning against the van. "I don't know exactly what to say to him," I admitted.

"Let me handle it," my mother said.

We walked up to Gunny. He didn't say anything. He just glared at us.

"Gunny, we were wondering why you didn't eat with us," my mom said.

Gunny sneered. "You can't always pick who you play with, but you *can* pick who you eat with," he replied curtly.

I frowned. I was having a hard time keeping my temper under control.

"Look," my mom continued. "Until the tour is over, we have to live together. Why not make the best of things? This sort of behavior is really kind of silly for someone your age. You're acting more like you're twelve than twenty-two."

Gunny's face flushed crimson. His features hardened as he glared at my mother. He stood up straight and said, "Listen, lady, why don't you go home to your knitting and butt out of this? What does an old bat like you know about the rock and roll business, anyway?"

That did it. I stepped in front of my mom and snapped, "Why don't you shut your big mouth, Gunther?"

"I told you not to call me that," Gunny said. My mom backed away. Gunny reached out and shoved me a bit.

"Boys! Don't!" my mom cried.

"Don't try that again, Gunther," I warned. Maybe I wasn't the best guitarist, but I was an excellent student in boxing class. I'd taken boxing lessons from Coach Clayton at the Riverdale Rec Center for a long time and knew how to handle myself in a pinch. I never looked for a fight, but I wasn't intimidated by anyone, either.

"Okay, wimp," snarled Gunny. "You asked for it."

He threw an awkward roundhouse right to my face. I heard my mom and the girls scream. I easily dodged Gunny's punch and blocked it with my left arm. Quickly I countered with a swift right that landed squarely on Gunny's jaw. He flew back and crashed into the side of the van. Slowly he slid down the van until he was sitting on the pavement.

"Are you all right, Gunny?" my mom asked. She bent over to look at him. Gunny rubbed his sore chin with his right hand.

"I-I'm fine," he sputtered. "Leave me alone!"

"I'm sorry I had to do that, Gunny," I said, "but you asked for it."

Gunny struggled to his feet. He sneered. "I've been hit harder than that when I played in punk rock clubs."

I shook my head. "I think this cuts it," I said. "You're through with The Archies, Gunny. You're out of the band right now."

"Hold it, buster!" Gunny ordered as I turned toward my mom. "I've got a contract!"

"So sue us," Jug said.

"You'll get your money for the gigs," my mom promised Gunny.

"That's right," I agreed, "you'll get your money, but you don't have to play the last two clubs."

"Oh no you don't," countered Gunny. "I know what you're all up to. You don't want me to play in Martinsville so I don't get a chance to perform for Jimmy Street."

"Huh?" said Reggie. He looked at me. "Jimmy Street? What's he talking about, Arch?"

Betty, Ron, and Jug all turned to me. I just stood there, feeling kind of stupid.

Gunny smirked. "They don't even know about the possible record deal, do they?" Gunny said. "You didn't tell them."

"Denny told me not to tell them," I fired back at Gunny.

"Is that right?" Gunny said. "So why did he tell me?"

"What record deal is he talking about, Archie?" Ronnie wanted to know.

"Denny probably told you because you're older," my mom told Gunny. "Denny told Archie not to tell the band about Jimmy Street coming to the Martinsville concert because he thought it might make you nervous."

"Oh, sure! That's a good one," Gunny smirked.

"It's the truth," I insisted. "He thought the band might feel pressured to do well, and get tense."

Gunny laughed. "They *should* be tense. After all, a possible record deal might be riding on their performance."

Jug looked at me. "You'd better tell us what Gunny is talking about, Arch," he said.

I nodded and explained everything. I didn't leave a thing out.

"So Jimmy Street is forming his own record label and is looking for new talent," said Betty.

"And he and Denny are going to scope us out at the Martinsville concert," exclaimed Reg. "Cool!"

"There's no guarantee he'll like us—or even that he'll be there," I warned.

Gunny folded his arms across his chest and leaned back against the van. "The chances are better he'll like what he hears if you have a top-notch lead guitarist," he said. "And besides that, Denny will be expecting to see me perform." He grinned. "So am I back in the band or what?"

Ron and Reggie exchanged worried looks. "We might stand a better chance of landing a recording contract if Gunny plays with us," Reggie said.

"That's what I think, too," Ronnie said.

"Does a recording contract mean that much to you?" I asked them.

"Isn't that why we formed the band, Arch?" Reggie asked.

I looked at Betty and Jughead. They shrugged. "I guess it is," I said.

"Maybe you should give Gunny another chance because of the contract," my mom said.

I took a deep breath. "Okay," I agreed. "You're back in the band." I paused. "But only for these last two gigs. When this tour is over, you're out of The Archies."

Gunny grinned. "That suits me fine. All I want is a chance to play for Jimmy Street in Martinsville."

"One more thing," I added.

"What?" asked Gunny. He moved toward the door of the van.

"You watch your step around my mom."

Gunny looked at me and then at my mom. He nodded and got back into the van.

"Let's go," I said to the rest of the band. "The sooner we get this tour over, the better."

Chapter 13

Our show at the Rockin' Horse went off without a single hitch. We opened with my new version of "Riverdale Rock," and the crowd loved it. That set the stage for the rest of our act. We gave our best performance ever.

Despite the fact that Gunny and I hadn't exchanged a single word during the show, he played exceptionally well that night. In fact, he was never better. I guess he was tuning up for our Martinsville gig. The truth was, Gunny's guitar playing really did add something special to our group. It was too bad that Gunny's personality detracted so much from The Archies. I resolved that no matter what happened, after the Martinsville show, Gunny Witherspoon and The Archies would go their separate ways.

After we left the Rockin' Horse we drove back to our motel for a good night's sleep. We'd leave for Martinsville in the morning. For a change, Gunny and I rode in the station wagon that night with my mom, while the other kids went in the van. Actually my mom insisted that Gunny and I ride with her. The car was deathly silent during the ride.

"I got you two together for a reason," my mom finally said as we drove along. "There's been bad blood between you two since you first met. Tomorrow is the last show of the tour, and I don't want to see it end with you two still enemies." Neither Gunny nor I spoke. Mom glanced in the rearview mirror. "If you can sing and play together onstage, the least you can do is talk to each other offstage. You're both talented young men who may go somewhere in this business someday. But despite what you may have heard, it's better to make friends than enemies on your way to the top." We were nearing our motel. "Now how about it?" she said. "Why not shake hands?"

Mom pulled into the motel parking lot. I looked at Gunny. I reached my hand over the seat. For a minute Gunny hesitated. Then he shook my hand. We didn't smile. We didn't say anything. We just shook hands. The car stopped. Without a word, Gunny released my hand, opened the door, and got out of the car.

I looked at my mom. "We may not have signed a peace treaty," I said, "but I guess the war is over."

The next morning at breakfast, we were talking about the Martinsville show. Everyone was at the table except Gunny, as usual.

"I'm really excited about meeting Jimmy Street," Ron said. "I can't decide what to wear tonight."

"No one said that we're going to get a chance to meet Jimmy Street," I said. Ron's face soured.

"Who cares about meeting Jimmy Street?" Jug replied. "I'm more excited about getting a recording

101

contract." Jug licked his lips. "One hit record would buy me a year's supply of pizza."

"Knowing how you eat, there's no guarantee of that," Reggie cracked. We all laughed.

"I'm not the least bit nervous about tonight," I told the others. I reached for the sugar and knocked over the salt and pepper shakers. "Well, maybe I am a little nervous and excited," I admitted. I picked up a pinch of salt and tossed it over my shoulder for luck. Fortunately no one was sitting behind me.

"Speaking of nervous and excited," said Reggie, "I think the pressure has even gotten to Gunny. He tossed and turned all night. He was so restless he almost kept me from sleeping."

"Notice he said *almost*," teased Betty.

"Speaking of Gunny," said Ron, "here he comes now."

Betty looked at me. "You guys aren't going to start throwing punches again, are you?"

"Didn't Archie tell you?" Jug replied. "They shook hands last night and sort of patched things up."

"Good," said Betty.

"I'm glad to hear it, too," Ron remarked.

"Good morning," Gunny said as he stopped at our table.

"Good morning," my mom replied. "Sit down and have some breakfast."

"I will, but first I have something to say," said Gunny. He took a deep breath. "This has been bothering me all night and I don't know exactly how to say it, but I do know where to begin." He looked at my mom. "Mary—I mean Mrs. Andrews—I'm sorry for the way I talked to you and for what I said."

His words shocked us—although we were glad to hear them. Most of all I think my mom was glad to hear them. "Apology accepted," she cheerfully replied.

Gunny turned to the rest of us. "I'd like to apologize to the band, too—and especially to Archie." He paused. "I guess I have been kind of a pain."

"You said it," remarked Jug. Ronnie jabbed him in the ribs with an elbow.

"After Archie and I shook hands last night, I got to thinking about how I've acted from the start." He sighed. "I guess I've been pretty selfish."

Jughead was going to make another comment, but a stern look from Betty silenced him.

"I told you once I'd never been in another band where the members really pulled together for each other, and I think that was one of the problems," Gunny continued. "I guess being older was part of the problem, too. I feel like the time for me to make it in the music biz is running out." He shook his head. "I've been doing this full-time for five years, and I've never gotten a real shot at the big time. I've gone from band to band without ever getting that break."

"I think we understand a little better now, Gunny," I said.

Gunny nodded. "I understand The Archies better now, too," he replied. "If you're going to make it, you're going to make it as a group, because you all stick together." He smiled. "You don't need a new lead guitarist to make you better. You already have what it takes." He turned to walk away.

"Yo!" I cried. "Where do you think you're going?"

Gunny turned to look at me.

"Sit down and have some breakfast with us," I invited.

"Yeah," said Jug. "Join us."

"You already have breakfast," Reggie reminded Jughead.

"So I'll have another," Jughead replied.

"Here," said Betty to Gunny. She and Ron squeezed into their side of the booth. "Sit by us." She patted the seat with her hand. Obviously Gunny's speech had even managed to soften Betty.

Gunny smiled and sat down beside her. "Thanks."

"No thanks necessary," I said. "After all, you're still a member of The Archies." I looked at Gunny and suddenly got a great idea.

Chapter 14

The Rock upon a Star club in Martinsville was the biggest and nicest place we'd played yet. When we first arrived, we weren't sure we'd be able to fill the club for our show. But word of our past successes must have preceded us, because people began to pack the place as show time neared.

About an hour before we were scheduled to go on, there was a knock at our dressing-room door.

"Come in," my mom called.

In walked Sid Matthews, the owner of the club, with our manager, Denny Diamond.

"Do you want to see this guy?" Sid teased, pointing at Denny. We all smiled and started to get up.

"You're packing the house, so I hope you put on a great show," Denny told us. "Give it your best shot," he added, winking at me.

"Is Jimmy Street here?" Ron blurted out. "Can we meet him?"

Denny's smile faded just a bit. He glanced at Sid and then at my mom and me.

"They know all about it," I said. Before Denny could reply I added, "Don't ask how. It's a long story." Denny looked at Gunny, who was fooling with his guitar.

Denny's smile grew bigger. He nodded. "Jimmy's here to give you the once-over," he admitted. "Right now he's sort of laying low so the crowd doesn't mob him." Denny glanced at all of the band members. "I hope you realize what a big chance this is."

"They do," my mom replied, speaking for us.

"Well, good luck," Denny said. "Knock 'em dead. I'll see you after the show."

"Good luck, kids," Sid added. They went out and closed the door behind them.

After they left, I turned to the group. I had something to say. I'd been kicking over an idea in my head since early that morning. Hearing Denny talk about what a big break this was had convinced me. "I want to change something in the act," I announced.

"Now?" sputtered Reggie. "We're going on in twenty minutes and you want to change something now?"

"What?" asked Ron.

I took a deep breath. "I want to do Gunny's arrangement of 'Riverdale Rock' at the end of the show. Okay?"

The room was silent. Everyone stared at me.

Gunny looked at me strangely. "You're doing this for me, aren't you?" Gunny said. "You're giving me a chance to shine for Jimmy Street."

"I'm suggesting it because I think it'll work," I answered. "If you happen to impress Jimmy Street with your solo, that's your business." I checked the faces of my friends. "How about it?"

"Fine," said Reg.

"Good," seconded Ron.

"Suits me," Jug chimed in. He looked at Gunny and smiled.

"Betty?" I asked. She was the only one who hadn't responded yet. Betty hesitated a minute and then smiled.

"I think it's a great idea," she agreed.

"Thanks," said Gunny. "Thanks a lot."

My mom grinned. "No time for thanks. It's almost time to go on, Archies." She opened the dressing-room door. We picked up our stuff and strolled down the hall, into the wings of the stage. We stood in the shadows as Mr. Matthews introduced us to the buzzing crowd.

"And now," he called, "The Archies!"

"Let's give 'em a show they'll remember," I said. Everyone nodded. I took a deep breath and led my band out onto the stage.

"Let's rock and roll!" I called to the crowd. We began to play. Right from the start, the house was with us. With the support of the audience we gave the performance of our lives. The whole show was like a dream. The crowd roared at everything we did and every note we played. Before I knew it, we were down to our last number.

"And now to put a lid on it," I shouted, "we're going to give you a little something called 'Riverdale Rock,' featuring a solo by our lead guitarist, Gunny Witherspoon." I looked at the band. "Kick it!"

Gunny was absolutely spectacular. I'd never heard anyone play better guitar. It was a once-in-a-lifetime performance.

"Riverdale rock! Rock! Rock!" I sang as we ended the number.

"Riverdale rock! Rock! Rock!" the girls echoed.

After a moment of stunned silence, the crowd exploded into a thunderous ovation of applause, hoots, and cheers. It was a moment that I knew would live in my memory forever.

After several minutes of standing before the appreciative audience, we managed to leave the stage.

"That . . . that was really something special," my mom said, half-stunned herself.

Mr. Matthews walked up to us. "Super show, everyone." He patted each of us on the back. "Super, just super," he repeated over and over. He looked at me. "Archie, Denny would like to see you and Gunny in my office." He looked at my mom. "Mrs. Andrews, you'd better come along, too."

Reggie did a double take. "What about us?"

Mr. Matthews raised his hands. "Denny said he wanted to see Archie, Gunny, and Mrs. Andrews," he responded.

I looked at my friends and shrugged. Gunny, my mom, and I followed Mr. Matthews to his office. When we reached it he opened the door for us but didn't enter the room. We walked in and he shut the door behind us. Waiting inside were Denny—and Jimmy Street.

"This is Archie Andrews, Mary Andrews, and Gunny Witherspoon," Denny said, introducing us. He motioned toward Jimmy. "I think you all know who this is."

"Yes," said my mom. "It's a pleasure to meet you, Jimmy." He smiled politely and shook hands with her.

"Great show, Archie," Jimmy said to me. We shook

hands. " 'Riverdale Rock' is real catchy. Did you write it?"

"Yes, I did," I said to Jimmy. "Thanks."

He nodded at me and turned to Gunny. "And you play a mean guitar, Gunny."

"Thanks, Jimmy," said Gunny.

Denny jumped into the conversation. "Jimmy has a proposition for both of you," he said.

"I won't beat around the bush," Jimmy began. "I need a new lead guitarist." He looked at Gunny. "The guy I had left the band to strike out on his own." He eyed Gunny more closely. "I think you could cut it, if you're free to leave The Archies. I like your style. What about it?"

Jimmy and Gunny both looked at me. "Gunny is a free man," I said. I smiled at Gunny.

"Thanks, Arch," Gunny said. He shook my hand. "Thanks for everything."

"It's settled then," Jimmy said. "Welcome to the Pack, Gunny. Denny will work out the details of your contract with us. Denny is going to be working very closely with me from now on."

I started to move toward the door. I was happy for Gunny, but a bit disappointed. Jimmy hadn't said a word about The Archies.

"Yo! Hold it!" Jimmy called. "That's not all." I stopped.

"Jimmy likes 'Riverdale Rock,' " Denny said. "He'd like to record it with his band."

I stared in disbelief. "Jimmy Street wants to record my song?" I said.

Jimmy nodded. "I'd have to do some minor revisions, but I think the song has the potential to be a hit," Jimmy said. "Are you interested in selling it to me?"

I looked at my mom.

"It's your song," she said softly.

I thought about all the hard work I'd put into the song. I thought about all the time the band had spent rehearsing it. I shook my head. "It's The Archies' song," I said. "I don't think I want to sell it to someone else."

"Don't be hasty, Archie," Denny said. "There could be a lot of money in this for you." He glanced at Jimmy. "We might be able to sweeten the pot by offering you a solo contract, Archie."

Jimmy nodded. "It would be on a trial basis, of course. If it works out, you could be on your way."

I thought of the stories Gunny had told us about other bands he'd played with. "What about my band?" I asked. "How about them?"

"They're good," Jimmy said, "but they're a few years away from being ready for the big time."

I smiled. "But you think The Archies as a group might have what it takes to make it sometime down the road?" I asked.

"Sure," he nodded. "If you keep at it, I might even give you another look a year or so from now." He looked at Denny. "Right, Denny?"

Denny studied me. He shrugged. "You're the boss, Jimmy," he agreed. "After all, it's your record label." Denny paused. "Well, Archie, what are you going to do? Are you going to take a sure thing and strike out on your own or wait and see what happens with your group?"

"I really want to record 'Riverdale Rock,' " Jimmy quickly added.

I sighed and shook my head. "I'm flattered by the offer, but I think I'll keep 'Riverdale Rock' and stick with my group. I know it sounds crazy, but I have my reasons."

"And I think I understand what they are," Gunny said, smiling at me. "I knew you were going to refuse. But I also know that someday The Archies are going to hit it big as a group."

"No hard feelings?" I said.

"No hard feelings at all," Jimmy replied.

Denny shook my hand. "You know, now that I'm working with Jimmy, I'll be too busy to handle The Archies anymore," he said with some regret.

"I know," I replied.

"Of course," Denny added, "all you have to do to get work now is call the managers of any of the clubs you worked at on this tour. They're all begging to have you back."

"I'll call them," I said. I looked at Jimmy. "Could I ask a favor?" I said.

"Sure," Jimmy answered.

"The members of my band would like to meet you," I said.

"Say no more," Jimmy replied. "Just lead me to them."

I opened the door. My mom and I walked out, followed by Denny, Jimmy, and Gunny. When I opened the door to our dressing room, Ron, Reg, Jug, and Betty almost freaked.

I introduced Jimmy to my friends, one by one. "You put on a great show," Jimmy said to them. "Keep up the good work."

I had to laugh. I think that was the only time I ever saw Veronica almost speechless. She was like putty around Jimmy.

"I met Jimmy Street," she muttered as the group prepared to leave. "He actually touched me."

"Me, too," sighed Betty dreamily.

I was even a little jealous over the way they acted.

"Come back to Sid's office so we can work out some details," Denny said to Gunny.

"I'll be right there," Gunny said as Denny and Jimmy left the room.

"Gunny is joining Jimmy Street's band," I said to my friends. They all rushed over and congratulated him.

"I just want to say thanks to you all," Gunny said. "It's been something else playing with The Archies." He paused. "I'll never forget any of you. And I know someday you'll make it to the big time."

Betty, Ron, and my mom kissed Gunny on the cheek. He actually blushed. He looked at me and then gave me a big hug. Then he turned and went out the door, shutting it behind him.

"What did he mean we'll make it to the big time someday?" Reggie asked me. "What about the recording contract?"

I glanced at my mom. "We didn't get an offer," I said. "Jimmy Street said we're still a couple of years away from being good enough."

"What do you mean a couple of years away?" Reggie exploded.

"Well, it's not my fault," I said.

"You're the leader of the band," Reggie argued. "Couldn't you work out any kind of deal at all?"

I hesitated. I could have told him that I'd been offered a solo deal, but I decided to keep that information a secret. "He said he'd listen to us again later," I added.

"Later?" Ron grunted. "Oh, great! What does he think I'm going to do, sleep in cars while on tour for the next year or so?"

"Hold it," Betty said. "Calm down. What's the big deal? So we didn't get the recording contract. We still have the tour deal with Denny, right, Archie?"

"Well . . . no!" I answered truthfully.

"Why not?" Jug said. "Did he dump us?"

"He didn't *dump* us, in the true sense of the word," I replied. I explained about Denny's new job with Jimmy Street. "We can still get all the work we want on our own," I added.

"That's right," Mom put in. "I'll even call the clubs for you."

"Don't bother, Mrs. Andrews," Reggie said. He gave me a dirty look. "I'm quitting to look for a real summer job. I don't think I want to be a rock musician anymore."

"Me, either," said Ron. "This hasn't worked out the way I thought it would."

"But you can't break up the band now," I pleaded. I looked at Betty and Jug. "Tell them, Jug. Tell them, Betty."

Betty shrugged. "Maybe it would be for the best," she said, smiling weakly. "I think we all need to back off from this for a while."

"You too, Jug?" I asked.

"I don't know, Arch," he muttered. "I guess we're all just tired. Maybe things will look different when we get back to Riverdale."

I looked at my mom. "Then I guess we'd better pack up and head for home," I said.

Chapter 15

We arrived back in Riverdale at about 4:00 A.M. on Sunday. Everyone's parents were waiting at my house when we got there. My mom wanted everyone to come in for coffee, but Reg, Ron, Jug, and Betty all said they were tired and wanted to get to bed. I knew better. They were mad about losing the recording contract and the second tour deal. I think they blamed me for what had happened. I guess they were suspicious because I never told them what happened during the meeting with Denny and Jimmy Street. They didn't know that the only thing I had to hide was the solo deal they'd offered me. I was depressed about the whole thing, considering what I'd given up for the sake of the band.

I slept until about noon that Sunday. When I got up and went downstairs I found my dad making brunch for Mom and me. "I bet you're starved," Dad said as I sat down at the table.

"Not really, Dad," I said. "I'm not feeling so hot. I think I'll just have coffee."

My father looked at my mother. "If I didn't know better, I'd swear you just lost your best friend."

"Four best friends," I corrected. "I think The Archies are breaking up as a group."

"Your mother told me about what happened," Dad replied. "I can't believe that The Archies are going to split up now, when they're on the doorstep of success." He looked me in the eye. "Maybe the group would feel differently if they knew you passed up a solo career to stick with them."

"Maybe I made a mistake," I said angrily.

"You know that's not true," my mom put in.

"I guess you're right," I admitted. Dad served me a cup of steaming coffee.

"Maybe your father is right about telling the others about the song and solo contract offers you turned down." Mom paused. "They're all coming over here today to pick up their checks for the last part of the tour. You could tell them then."

I shook my head. "No," I said. "If they want to disband The Archies, I won't stop them." I gulped down my coffee. "I don't even want to talk to them. When they show up, just give them their money and wish them luck for me." I got up. My mom glanced at my dad as I walked out of the kitchen.

I spent all of Sunday afternoon in my room, thinking about the music business. I was starting to wonder if I wanted to make a career of music. I'd almost convinced myself that I didn't when I heard the doorbell ring. I didn't budge, even though I suspected that it was someone from the band. I stayed put in my room when the doorbell rang several more times. After what I considered to be a safe amount of time, I went downstairs to get a drink, figuring everyone had left. My parents were in the kitchen.

"Did they pick up their checks?" I asked. I opened the fridge.

"Yes," my mom answered. "They've all been paid."

I took out a can of soda and opened it. "Did they ask about me?"

"Nope," said my dad. "I guess you're right, Son. It looks like The Archies are finished. I guess that means you're through with music, too."

I took a sip of soda. "Not necessarily," I said. "I've been thinking about that up in my room. No matter how hard I tried, I just couldn't convince myself to turn my back on music. I love it too much." I shrugged. "I guess I'll just have to go solo after all."

"If you're going solo, you'd better start practicing a new act," Mom said.

"Now?" I inquired.

"Why not?" Dad replied. "There's no time like the present. I unpacked the van for you early this morning. Your guitar and amps are in the usual place in the garage. Why don't you go out and play a bit?"

I shrugged. "Why not? Maybe it'll cheer me up." I walked out the door that led to the garage. I opened the side door and entered my practice space.

"It's about time," Ron called.

"Yeah," groaned Reggie. "How long do you think we're going to wait to start our regular Sunday-night rehearsal?"

"Let's go," said Jug. "I'm getting hungry already."

I couldn't believe my eyes. Jug was behind his drums. Reggie had on his bass. Betty held her tambourine, and Ron was at her keyboard.

"Wha-what are you doing here?" I sputtered.

"Waiting to rehearse," said Reg matter-of-factly. "How many times do we have to tell you that?"

119

"But aren't you mad?" I asked.

"We were," Betty said, "but we all decided we had too good of a thing to throw away." She smiled at me. "And when your mom told us about the offers you turned down just to keep The Archies together as a group, we knew for sure our band is destined for greatness. So here we are."

"As long as achieving greatness doesn't take too long," added Ronnie, grinning.

I walked over to my guitar just as my mom peeked into the garage.

"I'll make some snacks for after rehearsal," Mom said, to Jug's delight. "And tomorrow I'll call a few of the clubs you played at to set up some additional summer dates."

"Terrific," said Ron. "But no more sleeping in cars."

We all laughed. My mom turned and left.

"What should we start with?" I asked as I slipped on my guitar. "I know!" I looked at the band and smiled. It felt good to be back together. "We'll do our version of 'Riverdale Rock.'"

"A great choice, Archie," Betty said.

"Eat your heart out, Jimmy Street," cracked Reggie.

"Let's kick it, Archies!" I called. And we all began to play.

Betty Cooper, Baseball Star

Michael J. Pellowski
Art by Stan Goldberg

Hyperion Paperbacks

FOR MELANIE JUDITH

Chapter 1

"Ah! The smell of baseball is in the air," Archie Andrews announced cheerfully. He dropped his lunch bag on the table in the school cafeteria. Then he pulled out a chair and sat down between Reggie Mantle, Riverdale High's self-proclaimed class clown, and Jughead Jones, who could very well be the boy with the biggest appetite in America. Archie surveyed the group, which also included Moose Mason, Chuck Clayton, and Dilton Doiley. "Do you smell it?" he asked them.

Big Moose, who was the best athlete in school but not the brightest guy around, shook his head in puzzlement. "Duh, no, Arch," he replied. "I don't smell anything."

"What you smell is sauerkraut, Arch," said Jughead, chomping his bologna on rye. "They always serve hot dogs and sauerkraut for lunch on Fridays."

Archie made a face. "Not *that* kind of smell. Come on, girls," he said, looking at us. Archie craned his neck, inhaled deeply, and then exhaled. "Don't you smell it?"

I inhaled and then exhaled. I nodded at Archie. "I smell it, but Juggie is right. It's definitely sauerkraut."

Everyone laughed. "Great," Archie grumbled. "Now we have two comedians in Riverdale High— Reggie Mantle *and* Betty Cooper."

"Maybe Archie smells my new French perfume," Ronnie Lodge suggested. She placed her hand behind her head in a model's pose and smiled smugly. Veronica is the daughter of the richest man in Riverdale. She is also my best friend, even though she is my bitter enemy when it comes to Archie. Ronnie and I have been battling for his affection ever since grade school. Sometimes Archie dates her. Sometimes he dates me. It's one of those classic teenage love triangles.

"What is wrong with you people?" Archie complained. "It's not perfume, and it's not sauerkraut." He opened his bag and pulled out a sandwich.

"Don't look at me," said Reggie. "I used deodorant this morning." Again we all laughed.

"It's the smell of baseballs, bats, and gloves," said Archie, ignoring Reggie. "Baseball sign-ups are after school today."

"Duh, we know sign-ups are today. But what's that got to do with all this talk about smelly stuff?"

"Some people get spring fever," explained Chuck, whose dad is Riverdale High's baseball coach. "Archie gets *baseball* fever in the springtime. It affects his senses."

"That's for sure," Midge Klump agreed. She lowered the sandwich she'd been eating. "Archie thinks sauerkraut smells like baseballs."

Archie rolled his eyes. "Okay," he said. "I admit it. I'm crazy. I'm a certifiable baseball nut."

"We know that," Dilton agreed. Actually there

wasn't much Dilton *didn't* know. Dilton was a bona fide genius. "I guess that's why we voted you captain of the baseball team this season, Arch," he said.

Reggie groaned. "I still think I should have demanded a recount," he muttered.

Jug looked up from his lunch. "You only got one vote, Reggie," he said. "And we all know you voted for yourself."

Reggie made a face. "I always vote for myself. I voted for myself for most valuable player, too. I've yet to meet anyone else who deserves my vote." He went back to his salami sandwich.

Jug looked over at Archie. He pointed at a brownie that had spilled out of Archie's bag. "Do you want that, Arch?" he asked.

"You can have it, Jug." Archie and Jughead were an odd couple, but they had been true-blue buddies for years.

"Thanks, Arch," said Jug. He quickly grabbed the brownie. Jug always collected leftovers from other people's lunches. So far today, in addition to the brownie, he'd piled up two extra sandwiches, three snack cakes, a pint of milk, a couple of cookies, several pieces of fruit, and a bag of chips.

"You always were a baseball fanatic," I reminded Archie. "Even back in Little League you took the game more seriously than anyone else."

Archie smiled. "Little League sure was a lot of fun." He looked me in the eye. "I can remember when the best pitcher in the entire Little League was a skinny little blonde in pigtails, with a blazing fastball. I think her name was Betty Cooper."

I blushed. When I was younger, I had been one of

only a few girls in Riverdale who had played baseball with the boys instead of girls softball. I'd always loved baseball—I still did. Softball was just the next best thing.

"Betty was a pretty good shortstop, too," Midge said.

"Good?" Chuck remarked. "She was a human vacuum! She never missed a ball that went anywhere near her."

"Duh . . . and she could really hit," Moose added. "I remember once she hit two home runs in a single all-star game."

Jughead chuckled. "And they were both off Reggie."

Reggie grunted. "I took it easy on Betty because she was a girl," he claimed. "I still don't know why they let girls play Little League."

I glared at Reggie. "They didn't *let* me play," I said to Reggie. "I earned the right to play."

Chuck's girlfriend, Nancy, nodded. "Lucky for you Bernadette isn't here to hear that sexist remark," she said to Reggie. He had dated Bernadette Brownlee. She is a big supporter of equal rights for women—as are most of the girls in our group. But Bernadette is generally more vocal about her views than the rest of us are.

Reggie made a halfhearted attempt at an apology. "It's just that baseball is for boys, and softball is for girls," he explained, grinning at me. "That's why Betty plays softball in high school instead of baseball."

Midge glared across the table at Reggie. "Betty is

an all-league and all-county shortstop, which is more than you can say," she snapped.

"And our softball team won the league championship last year," Nancy added.

Ronnie nodded. "Where did the boys baseball team finish in the standings last year?" she asked innocently.

"We finished dead-last," Jughead answered, gnawing on an apple he'd bummed from Dilton. Jughead played right field on the baseball team.

"But we were in every game," Archie quickly added. "Except those two games against Southside High, when we faced Al 'Zippy' Zimmerman, the best pitcher in the state." Archie sighed. "Zimmerman mowed us down last year, but this year will be different," he vowed.

Archie was a second team all-league pick at second base. The only Riverdale player named to the first team all-league squad was Big Moose. Moose pitched when he wasn't playing first base.

"This year is going to be our year to challenge Southside High for the league title," Archie predicted. "This year we have a squad of veteran lettermen at every position except shortstop." Matt Gordon, last year's captain and regular shortstop, had graduated.

"Duh . . . we should have a great team," Moose agreed.

"I'll be at second base," Archie continued. "Jug will be in right field. Luis Martinez will be in center field. Chuck will be in left field and play first when Moose pitches. Reggie will be at third, and Eddie and Freddie Turner will handle the catching and fill in where they're needed."

"And don't forget me at shortstop," Dilton reminded Archie. Dilton had been the backup shortstop the year before and was in line to inherit the position this season.

Reggie chuckled. "You'd better watch out, Doiley," he said. "Betty just might come out for baseball this year and take your position away from you."

Instantly a worried look flashed on Dilton's face.

"He's only joking, Dilton," Archie reassured him.

"That's right," Chuck added. "Get serious."

Get serious? I thought. Could I seriously consider the idea? There was something appealing about it. I enjoyed softball, but baseball is just plain more fun. The idea of playing baseball in high school had occurred to me before, but I never gave it any serious consideration. I guess that's because in high school, girls are just expected to play softball. Reggie's remark started me thinking about it again. Maybe the idea wasn't ridiculous at all. I'm a good shortstop and the baseball team is without a strong backup at that position. Maybe I could help the team finally win a league championship.

Suddenly the bell rang. We hurriedly cleaned up our messes. I collected my papers, scraps, and wrappers and shoved them into my bag.

"See you later at the softball sign-ups," Nancy called to Midge and me as she left the table.

Ron quickly hurried over to Archie and hooked her arm in his before he could wander off. "Later, ladies," said Ronnie, leading Archie toward the exit and English lit. Archie almost tripped over a chair as Ronnie guided him away from the table. I knew she was fawning over Archie just to make me jealous. She knew Archie and I had a date that night, and this was her way of getting back at me.

"Bye, Betty," Archie called as he stumbled off. "So long, Midge."

"Bye," Midge replied. I didn't answer. I just waved and gritted my teeth.

When Midge and I were the last ones left in the cafeteria, she said, "I'm glad softball season is starting, aren't you?"

I nodded.

"You don't seem very excited about the prospect," Midge added as we walked toward the door.

"I am," I answered. "It's just that Archie's baseball fever might suddenly be contagious."

Chapter 2

In the crowded hall, Midge and I bumped right into Melanie Marks and Arabella Lane, who were also headed to gym class.

"Are you ready for softball sign-ups today?" Melanie asked Midge and me. Melanie was one of the best athletes in school. Her best sport was basketball, but she also played on the softball team.

"Absolutely," Midge replied as we neared the girls locker room. "We should have another great team this year." She looked at Arabella. "Why don't you try out for the team, Arabella? Softball is great exercise."

Arabella shook her head. "No, thanks," she answered. "Softball isn't for me. I'm thinking of trying out for the track team, though." Arabella had recently taken up jogging as a way to lose weight. Now she was addicted to running.

"Good for you, Arabella," I said.

"Do you think you can lead the softball team in batting again this year, Betty?" Arabella asked as we reached the gym and went into the locker room. The place was already filled with girls.

"She won't if I can help it," Melanie kidded. The

season before, I'd won the softball batting title by getting one hit more than Melanie.

"I'm not sure I can edge out Melanie two years in a row," I admitted. I took a deep breath. "Besides, I'm thinking of not going out for softball this year."

Melanie and Midge stopped dead in their tracks. "W-what?" sputtered Midge.

"Are you crazy?" Melanie asked.

I shook my head. "Actually, I was thinking about going out for a sport I like even better," I explained.

"Don't tell me you're going out for the track team, too?" said Arabella. She put her books down on the bench and opened her gym locker.

"I was thinking of going out for baseball," I replied.

"Baseball!" exploded Midge at the top of her lungs. "Betty, have you gone bonkers?"

Melanie stepped closer to me. She put a hand on my shoulder and looked me in the eyes. "Are you serious?"

I nodded. "Yup. I like softball, but deep down I really love baseball, and I think I'm good enough to help the team."

"But what about the softball team?" sputtered Midge.

I sat down and put my books beside me on the bench. I began to untie my sneakers. "The softball team really doesn't need me," I said. "Our team can win the league championship with or without me." I looked at Melanie. "Melanie knows that's the truth."

Melanie shrugged her shoulders and then nodded.

"We're a shoo-in," she admitted. She opened her locker and began to change for gym.

"But baseball is a boys sport," Midge blurted out.

Suddenly Bernadette, who was also in our gym class, popped into the aisle. She'd overheard our conversation from the next row. "Betty cannot be legally excluded from trying out for the baseball team just because she's a girl," she stated. "I think it's about time someone rocked the boat here in Riverdale." Bernadette nodded her head assertively. "I read about two girls in New York who played on football teams last year and another girl in Ohio who was a member of the wrestling team. It's about time Riverdale got liberated, too!"

"Hold it, Bernadette," I said, raising my hands. "Don't blow this thing out of proportion. I'm trying out for baseball because I like the sport and I think I'm pretty good at it. That's all there is to it."

Bernadette shrugged. "Whatever your reasons, I think it's great."

"So do I," Arabella agreed. "Go for it!" She and Bernadette started toward the gymnasium.

"Betty," implored Midge, "think about this. If you go out for baseball, the boys will freak out!"

"So let them," Melanie said. She closed her locker and walked away. Once again, it was just Midge and I.

Midge stared right at me. "Some of the other girls might not understand, either."

I stopped in the middle of changing. "What do you mean?"

"They might . . . well, they might think you're trying to be a show-off or a flirt," Midge said.

I laughed. "You know that is the farthest thing from the truth. You know how I feel about baseball." I leaned closer to her. "How many high-school girls besides me do you know who still have a baseball card collection—or ever had one in the first place?"

Midge held up her hands in surrender. "I know! I know!" she admitted. "I'm just trying to help you avoid the trouble I see coming if you sign up for baseball instead of softball."

I shook my head and closed my locker. "I think you're overreacting," I said. "Reggie might flip if I sign up, but he'll get over it. But can you actually see Archie, Dilton, or Jughead getting mad?"

Midge didn't answer. "I don't know," she finally admitted.

"Well, how about Moose?" I asked. "Do you think he'd resent it if I tried out?"

"He might," Midge said.

I shook my head. "I don't believe it. You heard what they said about me. I never had any problems when we played together in Little League." I thought for a minute. "Except with Reggie."

"That was then, and this is now," Midge countered.

At that moment Ms. Butler, our gym teacher, walked by on her way to the gym. "Let's go, girls," she urged. "Hurry up or you'll be late."

"Yes, Ms. Butler," I responded. Midge and I started for the door.

Midge stared at me. "You'd better think this over carefully," she cautioned. "If you try out for the baseball team, you're asking for trouble."

I couldn't believe Midge was making such a fuss about my idea. "Okay, I'll think it over," I said as we heard the whistle blow. We hurried out of the locker room into the gym.

I was at my hall locker after school when Ron, Nancy, and Judy Johnson came up to me. "Hi, girls," I greeted them as I collected the books I needed for homework. "Why the stern faces?"

"Tell me it isn't true," Ron demanded, looking me in the eye.

"What?" I shut my locker.

"This baseball nonsense." Ron kept her eyes trained on me as if I was a target.

"It's not nonsense," I replied.

"You mean you're really going out for baseball instead of softball?" Judy asked, as if the idea was totally preposterous.

I shrugged. "Maybe," I said casually. "Who told you?"

"Bernadette told me," answered Nancy, "and I mentioned it to Ron and Judy."

"Betty, this could be the sneakiest trick you've ever used to get close to Archie!" Ron snapped.

"What are you talking about, Veronica?" I said, shocked by her outburst.

"I'm talking about your being with Archie during baseball practice," Ron said. She waved a finger in front of my face threateningly. "You cooked up this crazy scheme just to spend extra time with Archie!"

My face flushed with rage. "How dare you!" I shouted. "If I do decide to go out for baseball, it will be because I *like* baseball, not so I can spend extra time with Archie or any other boy." In all honesty,

that thought had never occurred to me until now. "Besides," I continued, "if you're so worried about Archie, you can try out for the baseball team, too."

"Ha!" Ron scoffed. She whisked her long black hair off her shoulders. "I'd never stand a chance on the baseball team. Besides, who wants to get all sweaty and dirty playing baseball? I'd much rather get my exercise on the tennis court."

"What girl in her right mind would want to play baseball with the boys?" Nancy said.

"*This* girl wants to play baseball, and I *am* in my right mind," I snapped.

"I can't believe this," Judy said. "I thought it was a joke."

I looked at the three of them. "I can't believe that three people who are supposed to be my friends are acting this way," I retorted. "What I do with my life is my business." I turned to walk away. "If I want to go out for baseball, I will—and nothing anyone says will stop me." I was mad. I was disappointed in my friends. I turned my back on Ron, Nancy, and Judy and left.

"If you go out for baseball, you'll regret it," Ron called after me. "I'll never forgive you for this!"

Chapter 3

I stopped outside the room where the baseball sign-ups were taking place and took a deep breath. The hallway was deserted. School always emptied quickly on Friday afternoons. I could hear Coach Clayton speaking inside the room. I was late getting to the sign-up because I'd wandered around the empty building for a while after the confrontation with my three friends. I'd needed that extra time to sort things out and had finally come to a decision.

"It's now or never," I muttered to myself, stepping toward the open doorway. When I walked into the room, I found it packed with boys. Coach Clayton was seated on the desk at the front of the room. The boys were seated at desks or standing against the walls. Coach Clayton stopped talking when he saw me. For an instant the room was deathly silent.

"You've got the wrong room, Betty," Coach Clayton said.

I mustered my courage and smiled. "No, I don't, Coach," I answered, shaking my head.

The room began to buzz. Coach Clayton smiled indulgently. "These are baseball sign-ups, Betty. The softball sign-ups are in room twenty-eight." He pointed out the door.

Again I shook my head. I walked toward Coach Clayton's desk. "I'm not looking for the softball sign-ups," I clarified. "I'm here to sign up for baseball. I want to try out for the team."

There was a collective gasp from the boys in the room and then some laughter. Even Coach Clayton, who was usually unshakable, seemed to be caught off guard by my announcement. "D-did you say you want to try out for the baseball team?" he sputtered in shock.

"Sure!" I replied, looking directly at him. "There are no rules against it, are there?"

Coach Clayton shook his head slowly. He didn't look mad, but he sure was surprised. He pushed a sign-up sheet toward me. "Are you sure you want to do this?" he asked.

I nodded. I could hear some comments from the room, such as, "Is she nuts?" and "What's she trying to prove?" I pretended not to hear.

"Okay," said Coach Clayton. He smiled and tapped the sign-up sheet with his finger. "Put your name and position on this list."

I bent over and added my name and position to the long list. As I was writing, someone in the rear of the room shouted out. "Hey, Coach! You're not going to let some wimpy girl try out for our team, are you?" I looked up, but I couldn't see who it was.

Coach Clayton frowned angrily. "I don't want to hear any more remarks like that," he warned. He looked at me. "Okay, Betty, see if you can find a seat."

I nodded and walked over to the first row, where Dilton was seated. There were no empty chairs, so Dilton got up and gave me his.

"Thanks, Dilton," I said as I sat down.

Dilton didn't answer me. He glared at me for an instant, then collected his things and moved to the back of the room, where Archie and Jug were sitting.

I felt very uncomfortable—all eyes in the room seemed to be on me. I squirmed a bit in my seat.

"Let's get one thing straight," Coach Clayton told everyone. "There are no favorites on my team. I select my squad based solely on attitude and ability." He glanced around the room, and his eyes rested on his own son, Chuck. "If Chuck doesn't prove to me he deserves to be on this squad, he won't make the team—even if my wife kills me."

Everyone laughed.

Coach Clayton continued. "When I see you on the practice field, I judge you strictly by your talent, not by the fact that you're tall or short, black or white, junior or senior, boy or girl." He looked over at me. "The best players in this room will play for me."

I looked down and smiled. Coach Clayton had a reputation for being very fair. I knew I could count on him to give me a legitimate tryout.

Coach Clayton paused. "In here, we're all just ballplayers, understand?" He waited a minute. When no one replied, he spoke again. "Understand?" he said more loudly.

"Yes sir!" we shouted.

Coach Clayton nodded. "Good." He sat back down on the desk and studied the sign-up sheet. "We have a lot of players out this spring." He glanced around the room. "Only Archie, our captain, and Moose, last year's MVP, are assured a place on the team. All other positions are up for grabs." Coach Clayton stood up.

"That's all. See you at practice tomorrow, and don't think you can be late just because it's Saturday."

The room started to buzz again as aspiring players got up from their seats and made their way to the door. I went out into the hall and waited for Archie. Since we had a date for the movies that night, I thought he would offer to drive me home.

As I was waiting, Dilton came out. He stopped, stared at me, and then walked off without saying a word. Next, Reggie, Chuck, Luis, and the Turner twins came out in a group.

"There she is!" Reggie said, pointing. "It's Miss Macho, Betty Cooper!" He looked at his friends. "I hear she's going out for football after baseball season ends." The other boys laughed and shook their heads.

"Very funny, Reggie," I said.

"We don't think there's anything funny about this at all," Reggie answered. He and the other guys walked away.

Finally Archie came out with Jughead and Moose.

"Duh . . . see you later, guys. I've got to meet Midge. She's signing up for softball," Moose said, emphasizing the word *softball*. He glanced in my direction and walked off. Archie and Jug came over to me.

"Why did you do it, Betty?" Archie asked before I could even say hello.

I looked at Archie, puzzled. I had never expected *him* to question me about this. I figured he, of all people, would support me.

"Why did *you* sign up?" I replied, a hint of anger in my tone.

"Because I love baseball and want to play it," Archie said.

"That's why I signed up, too," I retorted.

"Good reason," said Jug. He took a candy bar out of his vest pocket and began to eat.

"But Betty," protested Archie, "you must have known this would cause hard feelngs. Dilton is really steamed. So are most of the other boys."

I shrugged. "And so are a lot of girls. But the truth is, I didn't think this would be a problem. It's not like we're living in the Dark Ages. I'm a girl who happens to like a sport traditionally played by boys. And I'm good at that sport. So what's the big deal?"

"It's no big deal to me," Jughead said, nibbling on his candy bar.

"Thanks, Juggie," I replied. "You're one of the few sensible people around here." I turned to Archie. "Now why don't you try being sensible, too?"

Archie sighed and stroked his carrot-colored hair. "I know you're a good player, and I know how much baseball means to you, Betty," he said, "but I honestly believe girls belong on the softball team."

"Oh, really?" I responded. "And I guess you feel a woman's place is in the home, too, huh?"

"I do not," Archie snapped. "I think a woman should be able to do anything she wants."

"Except play baseball," I said. "Well, maybe you'll be lucky and Coach Clayton will make me his first cut of the year."

"I doubt it," interjected Jug as he finished off his candy bar. "I happen to know you're better than a lot of the guys who signed up. You're probably better than some of the returning lettermen, too—including me."

I smiled at Jug. I had always respected the way he made up his own mind about things instead of simply following the crowd.

"Listen, Betty," continued Archie. "You've heard me talk about how important this baseball season is to me. This may be the best chance we'll ever have to win the league championship. I don't want anything to interfere with that."

I looked into Archie's eyes. "Maybe I can help the team win the championship. Did that ever occur to you?"

"All that occurs to me is that having you try out for the team will cause dissension," Archie answered.

I shook my head. "What would you like me to do, Archie, quit before I even try out?"

Archie nodded slowly. "I think that would be for the best," he said. "If you tell Coach Clayton you've changed your mind, you can still sign up for softball and everyone will be happy."

I thought for a minute. "*I* wouldn't be happy," I replied. "I really want to play baseball this year."

Archie seemed shocked by my response. He looked at me almost coldly and said, "In that case, you'd better get a good night's sleep tonight."

"What do you mean?" I asked, a bit puzzled.

"I mean, practice starts tomorrow and I don't think it would be a good idea if we went to the movies tonight. We both need our rest," Archie explained.

"Oh, I understand," I said, trying to hide my disappointment. I'd looked forward all week to spending an evening with Archie. "I guess you're right."

"I don't get it," said Jug. "Going to the movies was a good idea when Betty was trying out for the softball team."

His comment drew a frosty stare from Archie. "If you don't mind, we're talking personal business," Archie told him.

"Right, Captain!" Jughead said, saluting. "See you at practice tomorrow, Betty." He waved and walked away.

"I don't want to break our date, but I think it's for the best," Archie said.

"So do I," I lied. "The more rest I get, the better I'll play tomorrow."

Archie nodded. "Do you need a ride home?" he asked.

I shook my head. At that moment I wanted to be alone. "No. I feel like walking." I turned and headed toward the exit. I felt lonely, disappointed, and angry all at the same time. The empty halls of Riverdale High had never seemed so unfriendly before. It seemed as if almost the whole school was suddenly against me—and all because of baseball.

Chapter 4

That evening I sprawled on the bed in my room and cradled the portable phone against the side of my head.

"I can't believe you did it," Midge said, her voice booming out of the phone's receiver. "I still can't believe you actually did it. When Moose told me about it, I almost dropped dead. I told you the boys would freak out, didn't I?"

"Yes! Yes! You told me," I answered Midge. "But what did Miss Grundy say when I didn't show up at the softball sign-up? Was she mad?" I hadn't had a chance to tell Miss Grundy about my plans, and I wanted to make certain she wasn't angry. I really liked her—as a coach, a teacher, and a person. I hoped she understood my decision.

"Miss Grundy laughed and said, 'Good for Betty' when she heard the news. She also said that if any girl could make the Riverdale baseball team, it would be you."

I breathed a sigh of relief. "I'm glad she feels that way." I paused. "Are you still upset with me about this?" I asked Midge.

"Nah!" she said. "I realized this afternoon I was acting kind of stupid."

"I'm really glad you called, Midge," I confided. "I was sitting here brooding because Archie broke our date tonight. Talking to you has made me feel much better." I'd told Midge about Archie's reaction—actually, I'd spilled my guts to her the minute she'd called. I just couldn't keep my emotions pent up any longer.

"Don't worry about Archie," Midge reassured me. "He'll get over it. This baseball captain thing has just put a little extra pressure on him. He feels the team has to win the championship this year, or else."

"He should know by now that winning isn't everything," I said.

"You know how boys are when it comes to sports," Midge said. "Moose isn't fit to be around when the team loses a game."

"We like to win, too," I reminded Midge, "but we don't get all bent out of shape over a game. Maybe that's why our softball team is so successful. We keep things in perspective."

"Speaking of perspective," said Midge. "What did your folks say when you told them about baseball?"

I laughed. "My dad smacked his forehead with his hand and said, 'Here we go again,' " I answered, "the same reaction he had years ago when I told him I wanted to sign up for Little League."

Midge snickered. "If I remember right, your father never missed a single Little League game and was the loudest fan in the stands."

"Wrong," I corrected. "My dad was the second loudest. My mom was the loudest."

"That's right," Midge laughed.

"My folks are behind me one hundred percent, as

usual," I said. I was lucky. My parents have always been supportive of the decisions I make, as long as they're sensible. And, unlike some people, my parents were comfortable with my baseball plans. I changed the subject. "Is Ron still fuming?"

"Yes," Midge sighed. "She's convinced you're doing this only to be around Archie."

"If she knew how angry this is making Archie, she'd probably rejoice and be my friend again."

"She's still your friend," Midge corrected. "This is just another one of those Archie spats you two always have. It'll blow over."

"I guess," I said. I heard a *click.*

"I have another call," Midge said. "It's probably Moose. We're going to the movies."

"I guess he doesn't need any extra rest," I joked.

Midge laughed. "Hold on while I answer it." Midge went to the other call. After a few seconds she came back on the line. "It *is* Moose," she said. "I've got to go. Since baseball practice is in the morning and softball is in the afternoon, I won't see you at the field. Good luck, Betty!"

"Thanks, Midge," I replied. "I'll try my best. Good luck at softball practice. Tell all the girls I'm rooting for them."

"I will," said Midge. "Bye." She hung up. I put the phone on its cradle and lay back on my bed.

"Betty Cooper—baseball player," I said out loud. Despite all that had happened so far, I liked the sound of those words.

Chapter 5

The boys trying out for the team gave me the silent treatment when I arrived at practice the following morning. I didn't see Archie or any of my close friends, which made me think they were purposely avoiding me.

I changed into my playing clothes in the girls locker room, which was silent and deserted. Then I tugged on my cap and picked up my baseball glove. I put the glove on and pounded it with my fist. "We've got work to do," I said to the glove.

When I reached the field, I spotted Archie speaking to Moose, Reggie, and some of the regulars from last year's team. He saw me, too, but quickly looked away. I was really disappointed in the way he was acting.

"Morning, Betty," someone behind me said. I turned to see Jughead walking toward Archie's group.

I smiled my best smile. "Good morning, Jughead, and thanks."

"Thanks for what?"

"Thanks for being Jughead," I answered. He gave me a puzzled look but smiled anyway.

Suddenly Coach Clayton appeared with Eddie and Freddie lugging the baseball equipment out to the field.

"Okay, everyone, over here!" Coach Clayton shouted. Quickly we all gathered around him. "I want all of you to pair up and have a catch to loosen up your arms while I put out the bases," Coach Clayton directed. He pointed at the bag containing baseballs. As soon as Coach Clayton finished speaking, the boys started reaching into the bag to pull out the balls. As everyone was quickly paired up in twos, Archie and Jughead grabbed a ball and moved across the field. Reggie and Moose paired up. The Turner twins paired up with Chuck and Luis. By the time I got to the bag to take out a ball, everyone was already throwing with someone else.

I looked around. Dilton was involved in a three-way catch with two other boys. I was the odd person out, and I knew it was on purpose.

"What's wrong, Betty? No partner?" Coach Clayton asked when he returned from placing the bases on the field.

"I guess not," I replied.

Coach looked around at the games of catch going on and then back at me. "It's going to take a while for them to get used to your being here," he told me. "This isn't going to be easy for you, but I think you can tough it out." He smiled. "I've seen you play for the softball team," he continued. "Just give me one hundred percent and don't get discouraged."

I smiled back at Coach Clayton. "I'll give you a

hundred and fifty percent, and I won't get discouraged," I promised.

"Good," said Coach Clayton. "Now I suggest you convince one of those boys to have a catch with you." He turned and walked away. As soon as he left, I went over to Dilton.

"How about catching with me?" I said, bouncing the ball in my throwing hand.

"I'm already having a catch," Dilton replied. He caught the ball thrown to him by one boy and then tossed it back to the other boy.

"I thought you were a genius," I said to Dilton. "Do I have to define the term *pair up* to you? A threesome isn't pairing up, is it?"

Dilton caught the ball and threw it again. "Okay, Betty," he said, "I'll have a catch with you, but don't think this means I approve of your going out for the team." Dilton waved to the other boys and walked off with me.

"I'm not asking you to be my support group," I snapped. "I only want to play catch with you." I tossed Dilton the ball. He actually smiled at my comment.

"Okay, Betty," he said, returning the ball. "But don't think you're going to beat me out at shortstop."

I threw the ball back. "We'll see about that, Doiley," I remarked. "I plan to give you a run for your money." Dilton just nodded and fired the ball at me. I caught it and fired it back at him. We continued to play catch while Coach Clayton walked from group to group, checking out the throwing mechanics of each and every player.

153

"Good, Dilton," Coach said when he finally got to us. "Good, Betty. You've got a strong arm."

"Thanks, Coach," I said as I whipped the ball to Dilton.

After Coach Clayton finished making the rounds to inspect each pair, he called us together again, this time at home plate. "Put your gloves aside," he said. "I'm going to time each of you, running from home plate to first base. We'll race in pairs, so find a partner."

Here we go again, I thought. People quickly started to buddy up as Coach Clayton walked down to first base.

"Need someone to race against?" Archie asked.

I smiled. "Sure," I replied. "For a while there, I thought you were going to ignore me completely." Archie and I stood at the back of the lines that had formed behind home plate.

"I'm not ignoring you," Archie replied. "I'm just treating you like any other player going out for the team." He looked at me. "If you insist on trying out, I can't look at you and see Betty, the girl I go out with. I have to see a rookie shortstop trying to earn a place on the team roster."

"Fair enough, Andrews," I answered, moving toward the plate. Archie and I would be the last ones to race. By the time our turn came, all the others were at first base, near Coach Clayton.

"Hey, Arch!" yelled Reggie. "Leave her in your dust!"

"Yeah, Arch!" shouted Freddie. "Show her how to run."

155

Archie and I assumed starting positions on opposite sides of the plate. Coach Clayton raised his arm and then dropped it, to signal us to start. Archie and I bolted forward. We streaked down the baseline neck and neck and crossed the bag at exactly the same time.

"Wow!" said Coach Clayton, consulting his stopwatch. "You two really moved! Only Chuck and Luis were faster."

"It was a fluke," Reggie said. "Betty jumped the gun."

"I-I did not!" I puffed, between deep breaths.

"Maybe you'd like to run against her, Reggie?" Coach Clayton asked.

"Yeah, Reggie! Do it!" urged Eddie.

"Blow her away, Reggie," Chuck said. "You can do it!"

"Sure," said Reggie. "Let's go." He started toward home plate.

I caught my breath and started after him. We reached home plate and lined up on opposite sides. "This isn't Little League, Betty," Reggie said, glaring at me. "Get ready to lose."

I didn't answer. I got into position and looked down at Coach Clayton. He raised his arm and then dropped it. I shot forward with all of my might. I got out in front of Reggie right at the start and stayed there. I beat him to the base by four strides.

"Way to run, Betty," Coach Clayton approved. "That time was even better. You're only behind Luis now, and not by much."

"I-I was robbed," Reggie groaned. He held his side

with one hand and walked around. "I demand a rematch."

"Forget it, Reg," said Jug.

"Yeah," said Archie. "Betty beat you, fair and square."

"Duh . . . yeah," said Moose. "Betty sure can run."

"But it takes more than just speed to be a good baseball player," said Eddie.

"Right," seconded his brother Freddie. Other players nodded in agreement.

"Now," Coach Clayton announced, "I want half the team down at the batting cage, hitting against the pitching machine." Coach Clayton looked at Archie. "You run the machine, Archie. I have it set up."

"Yes, Coach." Archie started off toward the corner of the field, where the batting cage and pitching machine were located.

"The other half will stay here and I'll hit ground balls to them," Coach Clayton continued. He looked at Moose and Eddie. "Moose, you play first, and Eddie, you catch for me at home." The two guys nodded and went over to pick up their gloves.

Without delay, Coach Clayton divided the rest of us into two groups. I was in the batting cage group, which included Reggie, Chuck, and Jughead.

"Let's have a batter," Archie called out.

"Ladies first," Reggie said to me, bowing mockingly. He waved his arm toward the row of bats near the cage.

"Thanks," I said. I picked out a bat, put on a helmet, and stepped into the batting cage.

"Let's see how Miss Macho hits baseballs," Reggie

sneered. "They're a lot smaller than softballs, honey." The boys standing around the cage laughed.

I got into my stance.

"Ready?" shouted Archie.

"Let 'em fly!"

The first pitch came whizzing in. I swung with all my might—and missed. It landed against the back of the cage with a loud *thunk.*

The boys exploded with laughter. "I guess now she knows the difference between a baseball and a softball," Reggie cracked.

I ignored him and readied myself for the next pitch.

"Don't try to kill it," Archie advised. "Just keep your swing level and meet the ball."

The machine fired the next ball at me. I swung and drilled what would have been a line drive up the middle.

"Nice stroke, Betty," Jughead complimented me.

The next pitch came in. I smacked that one, too. *Whack! Whack! Whack!* I got three solid hits in a row before I missed another ball. When my turn at bat was over, I had hammered ten of the twelve balls pitched.

"Good work, Betty," Archie said as he started to reload the machine.

"Go for it, Mantle," I said, stepping out of the cage.

"Watch a pro in action," Reggie boasted. He picked up a bat and helmet and went into the batting cage.

"Here we go, Reg," Archie said. The machine delivered the ball.

"*Oof!*" cried Reggie as he swung as hard as he

could—and missed. He got back into his stance. "I'm just getting warmed up!" he remarked. He then swung at the next six pitches and missed all of them. He didn't even hit a foul. Finally he poked a few decent shots at the end of his turn. "I guess I'm a bit rusty," Reggie groaned, stepping out of the cage.

"More than a bit," Jughead cracked.

Chuck was next. He hit better than Reggie, but not as well as I had. Jughead went next and hit some really great line drives. One by one, everyone got a turn at bat. The last one to pick up the bat was Archie. Reggie ran the machine while he was up.

It quickly became apparent why the team had voted Archie captain. He looked good standing there with a bat. He looked even better hitting. He solidly whacked every ball pitched to him without missing a single one.

"Great hitting, Arch," Jug said.

"Super job," Chuck complimented.

"Way to go," I said as Archie stepped out of the cage. "You really know how to hit that horsehide."

Archie looked at me. "You're not too shabby with a bat, yourself," he replied.

"Hmph! Hitting against a machine isn't like hitting against a real pitcher," Reggie said. He glared at me. "I do my best when I'm facing a real fastballer on the mound. I can't wait to see how other people do in that situation."

Before the conversation could continue, the other group came running up to the cage. It was time to switch. My group headed back to the field so Coach Clayton could hit us ground balls. We quickly fetched our gloves and formed two lines. One line was at shortstop. The other was at second base. Chuck played first base, and Jughead caught for Coach Clayton.

Archie was the first player up at second. Coach Clayton hit him a sharp grounder, but Archie went far to his left, stabbed the ball, and fired it to first.

The first player up at short was Reggie, who usually played third base. He fielded the grassburner Coach Clayton hit to him and fired it to first. Reggie may have been a braggart and a wise guy, but as a fielder he was tops.

Other boys got their chances to field after that. Some made good plays. Some made average plays. Others made plays that were downright horrible. Balls were booted and bobbled, for errors.

When my turn came, Coach Clayton smacked a sizzling grounder deep to my right. I don't know if he hit me such a tough ball by accident or if he wanted to test me. I moved at an angle to cut off the ball and had to dive to stop it from going into the outfield. I stretched as far as I could and came up with the ball in my mitt. I quickly hopped to my feet and fired a perfect throw to Chuck at first.

"Super play, Betty," Coach Clayton called as I dusted myself off.

"Thanks, Coach." I got back in line.

"Good play, Betty," Reggie said grudgingly.

No one else said anything. No matter how hard I tried, I couldn't seem to break the ice. At that moment I doubted whether I could ever be an accepted member of the team.

I did well in fielding practice. I missed only one ball that I should have had. After we were all done, Coach Clayton had us run laps around the field. I ran my heart out and managed to stay at the front of the pack.

"That was good work for a first practice," Coach Clayton said. "I'll see you all on Monday after school. Moose, you and Chuck help me with the equipment. Archie, you and Jug close up the batting cage." Coach Clayton looked around. "The rest of you can head for the showers."

I picked up my glove and started back to the gym with the rest of the players. Most of the guys were talking about the way practice had gone. No one spoke a word to me. Dilton and Reggie walked by with the Turner twins and Luis, treating me as if I were invisible. It was a long and lonely walk back to the building. I showered and changed, taking my time. When I finally got back outside, most of the boys had left. Even Ol' Betsy, Archie's bright red jalopy was gone—Archie had left, too. For all I knew, he was on his way to a date with Ronnie. I shook my head and sighed. My love for baseball was sure causing problems.

Chapter 6

I spent Saturday night at home watching TV with my parents. My mom and dad are good company, but when it's a Saturday night and all of your friends are out having fun on dates, home isn't where you want to be. I went to bed early but didn't sleep well. I tossed and turned all night.

When I went downstairs on Sunday morning, I found my father at the kitchen table, his nose buried in the sports section. My mom was busy at the stove, making breakfast.

"Good morning," I said, sitting down at the table.

"Good morning, Betty," my mom answered.

My dad folded up the newspaper and handed it to me. "*Is* it a good morning? Here. You'd better look at this."

"What is it?"

"It's the local high school baseball and softball preview," he answered.

"Oh." I opened the paper. " 'Tis the season. It's in the paper about this time every year. I forgot all about it."

I quickly flipped the pages to the baseball preview. Then I saw it: a small column of text under the bold headline GIRL TRIES OUT FOR BASEBALL! I lowered the paper. My mom put our breakfast on the table and then sat next to me.

"You're a celebrity already," she said.

I looked back at the paper and began to read the article. "Betty Cooper, an all-league shortstop on the Riverdale softball team last season, has decided that playing hardball is more her style. When practice began at local high schools yesterday, Ms. Cooper was one of many candidates out for the Riverdale baseball team. Should she make the squad, it would be the first time in league history that a girl has ever played on an area baseball team."

I gulped and looked at my parents. "Oh, great! Now the boys are going to resent me even more. I wonder how the newspaper found out about this."

"News travels fast in a small town," my dad said. "Are you going to let it bother you?"

"No way," I said. I began to serve myself breakfast. When my plate was full, I looked at the main baseball preview. Most of the copy was about Moose and Archie, but Luis and Chuck were also mentioned.

I ate a hearty breakfast despite the newspaper piece and then helped my mother with the dishes. I spent the rest of the morning cleaning my room—it was a total mess. A bit after noon, Midge dropped by. When I opened the front door, she was clutching the sports section of the newspaper.

"I know!" I said, waving my hands in the air. "I already saw it."

"Oh," said Midge. "What did you think?"

"I think it stinks!" I remarked. "I had a difficult

enough time at practice yesterday. This will only make it worse."

"Absolutely," Midge agreed. "You know Reggie will flip when he sees it, especially since his name wasn't even mentioned in the preview."

I nodded. "I feel like drowning my sorrows in a milk shake. Let's go down to Pop Tate's soda shop. I'll buy."

"It'll be my pleasure," Midge said. Midge and I got into her car and rode off. During the drive I filled Midge in on the details of what had happened at baseball practice the day before. She reciprocated by telling me what had happened at softball practice.

"I think our team is going to be even better than last year," Midge said. She glanced at me and grinned. "No offense," she added.

"None taken," I replied. "I'm glad to hear it."

"Everyone was really hitting at practice," Midge continued. "Jenny Martin looked pretty sharp at shortstop," Midge added. Jenny was an infielder who had been my backup the year before.

"I knew the team wouldn't miss me," I said as we finally approached the soda shop. Midge parked and we got out. We saw Ol' Betsy and Ronnie's snazzy imported sports car parked nearby. "It looks like the gang is all here," I said as we started toward the entrance to Pop's.

We pushed through the door and stepped inside. In the rear of Pop's place, in one of the back booths, we saw a crowd of boys from the baseball team, hovering around Reggie and the Turners. Archie, Chuck, Dilton, and Jughead were all there.

Ron and Nancy were seated at the counter, sipping on sodas. The boys in the back were so busy chattering among themselves that they didn't even notice us.

"Am I allowed to sit here?" I asked Ron and Nancy, pointing at an empty stool. "Or do I have to go back there with the boys?"

"I don't think you'd be welcome back there," Ronnie said.

"Why?" asked Midge as she sat down.

"Because it's you they're talking about, Betty," Nancy answered. "They saw that article in the paper, and they're steamed."

I sat down. "Well at least you two are civil to me again." I looked at Ron.

"I guess I jumped to the wrong conclusion about this baseball thing," Ron apologized. "Now I realize you went out for baseball only because you really like it and not because you want to spend extra time with Archie."

Just then Pop Tate came up to take our order. Midge and I both ordered shakes.

"What convinced you?" I asked.

"Midge," said Ronnie. "She told me how the boys treated you at the meeting." Ron paused. "Not to mention what Archie said," she added.

"Archie?" I asked.

Ron nodded. "We went out on Saturday night and all he did was grumble about having a girl go out for the team."

"Terrific." I put my elbow on the counter and dropped my chin into my palm. I was driving the

boy I was crazy about right into the arms of my biggest rival.

Pop Tate came over and served us our milk shakes. "I saw the bit in the paper, Betty," he said to me. "I hope you make the team."

"Thanks, Pop," I answered. I unwrapped a straw and stuck it into my strawberry shake.

"I've only been out for the team one day, and already my life is almost ruined," I complained. I looked at Midge sternly. "And don't say, 'I told you so.'"

Ron looked at me. "Well don't let them make you quit now," she said.

My mouth fell open. "Huh?" I sputtered.

"They want to throw you off the team just because you're a girl, and that's totally unfair," Ronnie said. "It's malicious! It's spiteful! It's a dirty, rotten male chauvinist trick!" She sounded really mad. In fact, she sounded more like my crusading friend Bernadette than Ron, the girl who claimed she was born to shop.

"What's gotten you so riled up?" I asked. I was really surprised at her sudden change of heart.

"Do you know what they're doing over there?" Ron asked me. She pointed at the boys in the back booth.

"Looking at the latest swimsuit edition of a sports magazine?" Midge joked.

"They're writing a petition to submit to the school board," Nancy explained. "They want the board to say that only boys can be on the baseball team."

"What?" I shouted so loud that everyone in the soda shop—including the boys in the back—heard me. I slid off my stool and turned to face them. "Is there something you guys would like to say to me?" I called across the room.

Reggie slid out of the booth. He raised his hand and held up several sheets of paper. "We're going to let this do our talking, Betty," he replied. Reggie started to walk toward me. Archie, Jug, Dilton, and the rest of the guys followed behind. Reggie had an arrogant look on his face, but Archie and Chuck seemed a bit embarrassed.

"We saw that piece in the paper, Betty," said Reggie. "Thanks to you, our team will be the laughingstock of the league. We want you off our baseball team before the season starts."

"It's not *your* baseball team, Reggie," Ronnie snapped. "Athletic teams are funded by the school budget, which is created by taxes. The team belongs to everyone." Ron grinned. "And a lot of taxpayers in Riverdale are women."

"Look, Ron," said Reggie. "Boys aren't allowed to play on the girls softball team, so why should girls be allowed to play on the boys baseball team?"

"Reggie's right," Dilton agreed. "The rules are totally unfair—and prejudiced against boys."

"Baloney!" Nancy said. She, too, was now defending my decision to try out. "I didn't like Betty's choice at first, and maybe I still don't, but she has a right to make that choice nonetheless. This is America, guys."

"We're talking baseball here, not politics," said Archie. "All I want is what's good for the team. If having Betty on the squad is going to hurt the team, then she has to go."

"I can't believe I'm hearing this!" Midge said. "What a bunch of hogwash! Riverdale has male cheerleaders on its squad, doesn't it? Is there anything wrong with that?"

"And boys take home economics and cooking classes, don't they?" I added.

"Absolutely," Jughead quickly agreed. He'd been taking cooking class since he was in junior high school.

"That's different," argued Reggie.

"What's different about it?" I demanded.

"This," said Reggie as he waved the petition in front of my face. "Every boy on the team has signed it. We all want you off the team."

"Not *every* boy!" said Jug. He leaned on the counter. "I didn't sign it, and I don't intend to."

"Thanks, Juggie," I said. He tipped his cap to me.

"Moose signed it?" Midge sputtered angrily.

"Yup!" Reggie said.

"Just wait until I see him!" Midge vowed. "I'll give him a piece of my mind."

Nancy looked at Chuck. "Did you sign it, too?" she asked, pointing at him.

"Sure," said Chuck. "Why?"

"Because if you think girls should be excluded from some sports just because they're girls, you can take one of your baseball buddies to the movies tonight instead of me," Nancy snapped. She spun on her stool so her back was to her boyfriend.

"B-but Nancy," pleaded Chuck.

"Don't be intimidated, Chuck," Dilton urged. "Stick to your guns."

I looked at Archie. He fidgeted a bit. "I can't believe you signed that petition, Archie," I said. "That really hurts me."

"I didn't do it to hurt you, Betty," Archie said. "I did it for the good of the team. Please understand. And don't be mad!"

"Don't be mad," I sputtered. "How can I not be mad? Archie, I never thought I'd hear myself say this . . . but don't call me for any dates until this mess is all sorted out!" I couldn't believe those words had tumbled off my tongue. I turned to Ron. I had just about delivered Archie into her waiting arms.

Ronnie looked at me, then glanced at Archie. She took a deep breath and came to my side. She put her arm around my shoulders. "And that goes for me, too," she told Archie.

I couldn't believe my ears. Ron was my best friend, but I never expected her to make a sacrifice like that.

"Okay," said Archie. "There's nothing left to talk about."

"Let's go, guys," Reggie said. Everyone but Jughead left.

"It looks like the battle lines are forming," Jughead remarked.

"And our love life is the first casualty," groaned Ronnie. She looked at me. "Baseball sure must mean a lot to you."

"It does," I replied.

Pop Tate walked up to us. "I think there's more than baseball at stake here, girls," he said. "And I want to congratulate all of you. You're doing the right thing." He walked away.

Chapter 7

The next three days of school were tough, to say the least. Jughead had spoken the truth when he'd said battle lines were being formed. It seemed that everyone in Riverdale High, staff or student, had an opinion about my trying out for the baseball team. Some teachers, like Miss Grundy, openly supported me. She offered to help me in any way she could. Other teachers were very much opposed to my position. Mr. Dobson, a shop teacher and freshman football coach, came right up to me and told me he thought I was disgracing myself and Riverdale High.

What bothered me was the way the sides were being chosen. Most of the students who supported me were girls; most of the students who were against me were boys. That glaring difference was shockingly illustrated in the cafeteria, at our lunch table. Instead of sitting together as a mixed group—the way we used to—the boys now huddled together at one end of the table while we girls sat at the other end. Bridging the two groups were Jughead, who was walking a tightrope between the sides, and Moose and Midge, who had been boyfriend and girlfriend for so long, they didn't let outside issues interfere with their relationship.

For me the worst thing of all was baseball practice itself. The boys treated their equipment better than they treated me. Reggie and the Turner twins had a nasty remark ready at all times. The other boys tolerated me, but mostly by just ignoring my presence. Dilton or Archie would pair up with me when I needed a partner, but even they weren't overly friendly. Only Jughead treated me like a friend and a teammate. If it hadn't been for him, I probably wouldn't have been able to get through practice at all. As for the petition, I didn't know what became of it. The boys hadn't mentioned it since shoving it in my face on Sunday. Even Moose, who usually couldn't keep a secret from Midge, hadn't said a word.

"Have you heard anything about that petition?" Ronnie asked me as we changed for practice Wednesday after school.

I shook my head. "Maybe the boys forgot about it."

"They didn't forget about it, I can guarantee that," Bernadette put in. She was in the locker room, too, changing for track practice. "I know Reggie better than that," Bernadette continued. "He's probably cooked up something sneaky, so stay on your toes, Betty. And remember, we're behind you one hundred percent."

"That's right, Betty," Arabella called out. Soon all the girls in the locker room were echoing their support of me.

Bernadette's comment about Reggie rang a bell. Reggie wasn't the type to just forget about the petition. He was probably waiting for the right time to use it.

Suddenly it dawned on me. "Coach Clayton is making his cut list Thursday," I said out loud.

"Huh?" said Midge. "What did you say?"

"Reggie hasn't come forward with the petition yet because he's waiting to see if I get cut on Thursday," I explained.

"I get it," Ron said. "He won't need the petition if Coach Clayton cuts you from the squad."

"He's just biding his time, the sneak," Nancy added. She slammed her locker.

Ronnie stood up. She was all set for tennis team practice. "What are your chances, Betty?" she asked. "Are you going to make the team?"

I shrugged. "I think I've been doing well, but who knows? Today's practice will be very important."

"Why is that?" Nancy asked.

"Today we're going to face live pitching in a controlled scrimmage," I replied. "Coach Clayton will probably make his final decision based on what he sees today."

Midge flopped on the bench. "And Moose is pitching today," she sighed. "He's been looking forward to it." She looked at me. "Moose is going to try to make you look bad today, Betty," she warned. "I'm sure of it."

Melanie, who had been listening to our conversation, joined in. "Can you hit Moose, Betty?" she asked.

"I can try," I said. "He doesn't scare me, if that's what you mean."

"He'd scare me," Nancy admitted. "I bet he can throw that ball one hundred miles an hour."

"Only ninety," Midge corrected. "They clocked him last year."

"Well, now, that's a big difference," Arabella joked. She patted me as she started to walk out of the locker room. "You should be able to hit him easily, Betty." Everyone laughed.

"No problem," I kidded as people started to leave the locker room. Melanie was still standing there.

"I wanted to talk to you alone for a minute," she said.

"Sure, Mel," I answered. "What is it?" We started walking toward the rear exit.

"I wanted you to know I think you're terrific," she said. She stopped me before I could interrupt. "Let me finish. What you're doing takes real courage. I always thought about trying out for the boys basketball team, but I never had the gumption to do it. I just want you to know I admire you." She held out her hand. I shook it.

"Thanks, Melanie," I said. "That means a lot to me."

We walked out the door together. "By the way," she said before we separated to go to our respective practice areas, "smash one off Moose for me." She smiled and walked off.

I made my way to the baseball field. When I arrived, most of the boys were already playing catch. I looked around.

"Want to have a catch, Betty?" Archie asked me. I was a bit surprised by his offer.

"Sure," I responded. We started to walk off to one side.

"You know, Betty," he said to me in a timid sort of way, "I feel really bad about the things that have happened since you came out for the team."

"Not as bad as I feel," I replied.

Archie nodded. "I just want you to know the whole situation has been very difficult for me. I'm not really sure how I feel."

"Me, either," I said, looking him in the eye. We'd been avoiding each other in school and hadn't even spoken to each other on the phone. "But I guess I can understand your position. You're captain of the team, and you want to win."

Archie shrugged. "I keep thinking about what you said to me when you first signed up."

"What's that?" I asked.

"That maybe you can help us win the championship. And if that's the case, then you *should* be on this team."

"Thanks, Archie," I said. "Who knows? Maybe everything will work out in the end. Now let's warm up."

Shortly after Archie and I began to play catch, Coach Clayton called us all together. "This afternoon we're going to have a controlled scrimmage," he announced. "The way you play today will help me decide whom to keep on the team. Good luck to everyone." Coach Clayton then designated Archie to play second base, Dilton shortstop, Chuck first, and Reggie third. The outfield was made up of Jughead, Luis, and Eddie. Eddie's brother Freddie was the catcher.

"Moose will pitch first," Coach Clayton directed. "Tom Snyder, you'll be up first. Bill Morgan, you're next." Coach Clayton looked at me. "Betty, you'll bat after Bill." He continued selecting batters, making sure everyone who wasn't in the field would get a chance to bat.

I walked over and selected a helmet and a bat. I watched Big Moose loosen up on the mound. He was throwing hard. His ball flew to the plate and seemed to explode into Freddie's catcher's mitt.

"Hitting him is going to be tough," I heard Tom say to Bill.

"Let's have a batter," Coach Clayton called. He was standing on the mound, behind Moose. "I'll call balls and strikes from here."

Tom stepped up to the plate. Big Moose went into his windup. The first pitch was a high inside fastball. It was so close to Tom that he dropped to the ground to avoid getting hit.

"Ball one!" shouted Coach Clayton. He looked at Moose. "Settle down," he told him.

Tom got back to his feet, a bit shaken. He swung at the next ball and missed. In fact, by the time Tom had swung, the ball was already in Freddie's mitt. Tom took the next pitch for a called strike.

"You're looking good, Moose," Coach said. Then he turned to Tom and advised, "Swing quicker, Tom."

Moose got ready to fire. He burned one into the plate. Tom swung late again.

"Strike three!"

Bill stepped up to the plate next. "That guy isn't human," Tom complained as he walked past me.

"Strike one!" Coach Clayton called.

"Way to go, Moose," Archie shouted from second base.

"Breeze it by him," Dilton shouted.

Moose made his second pitch. Bill fouled it off for strike two.

"Now you've got him," Chuck shouted, pounding his first baseman's mitt with his hand.

Moose went into his windup. The ball whizzed from his hand and into Freddie's glove before Bill had moved a muscle.

"Strike three!" Coach shouted. "Next batter!"

Bill grumbled as I walked by him. I stepped up to the plate and dug in with my back foot.

"Well . . . well, look who's up," Freddie said, laughing. "Turn up the heat on that fastball, Moose."

I looked at Moose and saw him smile smugly.

"No batter!" Reggie shouted from third. "Don't waste any pitches, Moose."

I got into my stance and trained my eyes on Moose. He fired a good pitch right down the middle. I swung my hardest—and fouled the ball up and out of play, behind the backstop.

"Good swing, Betty," Coach Clayton said. I nodded and got back into hitting position. I was determined to hit that ball. I wasn't going to let Moose intimidate me.

The next pitch was a chest-high fastball. I swung and again fouled off the pitch. But at least my timing was good. I wasn't swinging late.

"Two strikes! Now you've got her!" Dilton shouted to Moose.

"Blow her away, Moose," Reggie called. "Show her what you can do."

The next pitch was low and in the dirt. I didn't swing. "Ball one!" Coach yelled. Moose gave me a mean look. He went into his windup and fired. I took the pitch. "Ball two!" Coach Clayton shouted.

"Don't lose her," Archie encouraged.

I got ready again.

"Oof!" Moose grunted as he launched a rocket in my direction. I swung and connected. The ball jumped off my bat and jetted toward deep left field. I dropped my bat and raced for first. Center fielder Luis hustled after the line-drive shot, but the ball kept going and cleared the fence for a home run.

"Way to hit, Betty!" Coach Clayton called as I circled first. I saw Moose frown.

"Nice hit," Archie said as I passed him.

I rounded second and headed toward third. "Dumb luck," Reggie grunted as I touched third and headed for home. I touched the plate and found no one waiting there to congratulate me. I was still the outcast. I walked over to the bench and sat down while the next hitter strolled into the batter's box to face Moose. What do I have to do to get these guys to accept me? I wondered as I sat there.

Chapter 8

On Thursday morning Midge picked me up and drove me to school. I had asked her to do me that favor. I wanted to get to school early. The final team list would be posted on the gym bulletin board bright and early. Since I'd done well in the scrimmage game, I felt confident my name would be on that list. But in case it wasn't, I wanted to be the first to find out the bad news.

"I've got my fingers crossed for you," Midge said as we walked down the back hall toward the gym. The hall was practically deserted.

"Thanks, Midge," I said, too nervous to talk much. My stomach felt like it was twisted into a knot. We reached the bulletin board.

"There it is!" Midge said. She pointed at the large sheet of paper tacked to the board. At the top of the paper, RIVERDALE HIGH BASEBALL TEAM was typed. "I can't look," Midge said, covering her eyes.

I took a deep breath and began to scan the sixteen names on the list. "A. Andrews, R. Mantle, M. Mason, J. Jones, D. Doiley, C. Clayton, L. Martinez," I muttered, going down the list. I read on. Freddie and Eddie Turner were on the list, as were Bill Morgan and Tom Snynder. When I got to the next name I stopped reading. "B. Cooper!" I exclaimed loudly. I tapped the paper with my finger. "B. Cooper!" I yelled again to Midge.

Midge shrieked, bouncing up and down in excitement. "Congratulations, Betty! You did it!" We hugged each other and jumped up and down.

"I'm on the team!" I cried. "I'm really on the baseball team." I stopped bouncing and raised a fist into the air victoriously. "Yes!"

Midge and I started back down the hall. We turned a corner and walked right into Jughead. "Juggie!" I shouted. "Did you see the baseball list?"

He nodded. "Congratulations, Bets," he said. "I knew you'd make the team."

I smiled. "I can't wait until Archie finds out," I remarked. "Won't he be surprised!"

"He already knows," Jughead said. My smile started to fade. I looked at Jug questioningly. "All the guys on last year's team already know," he explained. "We were here when Coach Clayton put up the list. We all came to school early just for that purpose." Jug corrected himself. "Actually I just tagged along because Archie's my ride to school."

Midge put her hands on her hips. "So that's why Moose told me he'd meet me at school today instead of picking me up," she said.

"But why?" I asked Jug. "I don't understand."

Jug pushed his hat back off his forehead. "The petition, Betty," Jughead answered. "They wanted to know if they would have to use the petition or not."

I nodded and glanced at Midge. I shook my head.

I'd made the team, but the real challenge was just beginning.

"That was a good practice," Coach Clayton said after we had finished running laps. "Again I want to congratulate all of you on making this year's squad. Our season opens next week, and I honestly feel we have an excellent chance at the league championship, *if* we play together as a team." He glanced at the group of sweaty players (including me) crowded around him. "With a total team effort, we can go a long way," Coach emphasized again.

Some of the players nodded. I wondered how they could agree with Coach Clayton's team message when they still refused to accept me as a teammate. I guess the guys thought if they continued to ignore and insult me, I just might quit. They still didn't know that Betty Cooper wasn't a quitter. I was on the team to stay.

"Okay, everyone," Coach concluded. "That's it for today. See you all tomorrow." The players started walking back to the building. As usual I walked alone.

"Hey, Betty!" Archie called. "Wait up." I stopped and waited for him to catch up. Archie hadn't said two words to me since congratulating me for making the team at the start of practice.

"You heard what Coach Clayton said about team unity," he began.

"Sure," I answered. "Why?"

"I just want you to understand that I feel—"

I stopped and raised my hands in frustration.

"Hold it, Archie!" I said angrily. "I'm getting a little tired of your explanations. If you want to win so bad that you think it's worth getting me kicked off the team for no good reason, go ahead and do it!" I was through with my teammates' juvenile behavior, tired of feeling uncomfortable and unwanted.

"Coach Clayton thinks I'm good enough to be a part of this team," I continued. "He's the same guy who evaluated you, isn't he?" I pointed at Archie.

As the other players approached I pointed at them one by one. "I've known all of you since we were kids, and this is the first time I've been ashamed to call you my friends," I said. "In fact, the way all of you—except Jughead—have been acting, I'm not sure you really are my friends."

A few guys looked away in embarrassment but I kept right on.

"Just who do you think you are, anyway?" I looked directly at Archie. "How would you like it if the guys wanted you off the team just because you have freckles?" I asked. I turned to Chuck. "Would you like it if they wanted to cut you from the squad because you're black?" I pointed at Dilton. "Maybe there should be a rule that players who have high IQs shouldn't be allowed to play." I looked around, and my glance fell on Reggie, who was glaring at me. "Oh, what's the use?" I stormed off toward the building.

When I reached the building I saw Miss Grundy standing with Mr. Weatherbee, the school principal. They seemed to be waiting for me.

"Betty!" Mr. Weatherbee beckoned. "I need to speak to you."

"Yes, sir," I answered. "Hi, Miss Grundy." I walked up to them. "What is it, Mr. Weatherbee?"

"It's about a petition the boys on the baseball team gave me to submit to the school board," Mr. Weatherbee explained.

"Oh, that!" I groaned, rolling my eyes.

"So you know about it?" Miss Grundy asked.

I nodded.

"Unfortunately, Betty," said Mr. Weatherbee, "the superintendent of schools is very concerned about this. When I gave him the petition today, he scheduled a special emergency meeting of the school board tomorrow night to discuss the matter."

"Wonderful," I muttered.

Miss Grundy put her hand on my shoulder. "Don't worry, Betty," she reassured me. "If you'll let me, I'd like to go to that meeting and speak on your behalf."

I looked up at Miss Grundy. She smiled at me and I smiled back.

"Don't be upset about this," said Mr. Weatherbee. "I'm sure the board will make the right decision."

"You mean they can overrule Coach Clayton?" I said.

Mr. Weatherbee nodded. "They could," he said, "but if I have anything to say about it, they won't." He, too, smiled. Mr. Weatherbee was rooting for me, I realized. "The bad news," he continued, "is that you won't be able to practice with the team again until the board makes a final decision on this tomorrow night."

I gritted my teeth. I wouldn't be able to practice with the squad tomorrow. Reggie and his buddies had finally managed to get rid of me—even if it was for only one day.

"It's only one day, Betty," consoled Miss Grundy.

"It's only one day *if* the board decides I can still play on the team," I corrected. I looked toward the baseball field. The boys on the team were approaching. "My parents and I will be at the meeting," I assured Mr. Weatherbee. I tucked my glove under my arm and walked into the girls locker room, before the boys got any closer. I didn't want them to see the tears welling up in my eyes.

I was still sniffing when I walked into the locker room.

"Betty, what's wrong?" Midge asked when she saw me. It didn't take much prodding from Ron and Midge and the rest of my friends before I told them about the school board meeting.

Bernadette stood up on a bench. "We can't let Betty go to that meeting alone," she stated. The room began to buzz. "We have to show the school board where we stand on this issue."

"We won't let the boys get away with this!" Nancy vowed.

"Don't worry, Betty," Melanie put in. "We're all behind you."

I wiped a tear that had trickled out of my eye and onto my cheek. It felt good to have friends on my side.

Ron came over and put her arm around me. "I'm with you, Betty," Ron said to me. "I have a manicure appointment tomorrow night, but I'll skip it to go to the meeting."

I smiled. For Ron that was the ultimate sacrifice.

Chapter 9

"Baseball for Betty Cooper! Baseball for Betty Cooper!" Bernadette cheered as she held up a sign imprinted with those exact words.

"Baseball for Betty Cooper!" the rest of the crowd of girls chanted.

My mom and dad smiled at me as we walked toward Riverdale High School. "You didn't tell us you were bringing your own fan club," my dad remarked.

"I didn't know about this," I said. "My friends told me they'd be here to support me, but I had no idea this is what they meant."

I looked at the crowd of girls and saw Midge, Nancy, Ronnie, Judy, Arabella, and lots of other girls from school.

"Here she comes now," Ronnie shouted, pointing at me. The girls cheered and applauded.

"Thanks, everyone," I said. "Thanks a lot."

Bernadette, Midge, and Ronnie came up and said hello to my folks. "We want Superintendent Harper and the school board to know how we feel about this issue," Bernadette explained to my mom.

"We feel Betty has earned the right to be on the baseball team," said Ronnie.

"So do we," my mom agreed.

My dad tugged on his tie, which he'd tied a bit too tight. "I just hope we can convince the school board of that," he said.

"I'm certain we can," replied Bernadette.

"We sure can," Midge agreed. She looked at me. "We'll see you inside."

I nodded. We walked into the building as the girls, led by Bernadette, began to chant again. We went through the deserted halls, into the auditorium where the school board held its public meetings. The board members were already seated at a table in the middle of the stage. The only other people in the auditorium so far were Mr. Weatherbee, Miss Grundy, and Coach Clayton. It was one of the few times I had seen Coach Clayton in a suit. They all rose as soon as they saw us, and we exchanged greetings.

"I'd like to introduce Betty to Dr. Harper and the board before the meeting starts," Mr. Weatherbee said.

My parents nodded. Mr. Weatherbee walked me over to the table and presented me to Dr. Harper and the members of the school board. On the table I noticed copies of the boys' petition and the newspaper article about me.

"Well, Betty," said Mrs. Van Nest, the board president, "I want you to understand that this is an informal meeting to determine whether this issue needs to be placed on the agenda for the board's regular meeting in two weeks."

Just then we heard a loud commotion outside. There was a chorus of boos.

"What is that?" asked Dr. Harper.

The answer to his question came soon enough. In walked all the members of the baseball team, dressed in their best suits. Reggie led the group, and Archie brought up the rear. Jughead wasn't with them. Meetings just weren't his thing. He was probably at Pop Tate's, munching on a pizza. The boys sat down on the far side of the room.

Right on the heels of the boys came the girls, led by Bernadette. They sat on the other side of the room, across from the boys.

Several teachers began to trickle in behind the girls, and soon the room had filled up. Mr. Weatherbee and I went back to our seats. I sat down between my folks.

About a minute later, the meeting was called to order. Mrs. Van Nest began to speak. "We're holding this meeting tonight to discuss an issue concerning high school athletics," she said. She picked up the newspaper clipping about me and held it up for the audience to see. "For the first time in our league's history, a girl has tried out for—and made—the baseball team." She put down the article and looked at Coach Clayton. "Coach Clayton," she asked, "are there any league rules that prohibit girls from playing on the team?"

He stood up. "No, Mrs. Van Nest," he answered. "Any girl can legally play on a baseball team, if she's good enough to make the squad."

"Is Betty Cooper good enough?" a board member asked.

"She's an outstanding player, in my opinion,"

Coach Clayton said. His comment caused a buzz among the boys.

"Thank you, Coach Clayton," Mrs. Van Nest said. She looked toward the boys. "Even though this is an informal meeting, I'll expect polite behavior from everyone in the room. Everyone will get his or her chance to speak."

Mr. Weatherbee raised his hand and was recognized. "Mrs. Van Nest, Dr. Harper, and members of the board," he began. "I've known Betty Cooper for most of her life. An individual of her caliber would be an asset to any team."

Mr. Weatherbee sat down.

Miss Grundy was recognized. "I had the good fortune to coach Betty Cooper in softball," she said. "I hate losing her to baseball, but it's obvious to me that an athlete of her ability can contribute to any sports program. Removing her from the baseball squad now would not only be a disservice to her but to the team and to Riverdale High as well." Miss Grundy sat down.

My dad spoke next. "My daughter deserves to be on this team," he said. "My wife and I wholeheartedly support her decision to play baseball." He looked over at the boys, and at Archie in particular. "Why the boys don't want her on the team is a problem they need to work out for themselves. We've always encouraged Betty to challenge herself and work through any obstacle—we are very proud of her." He sat down.

Mrs. Van Nest picked up the petition. "Apparently the boys feel that having a girl on the team will destroy team spirit and subject the team to ridicule," she replied. "They must feel very strongly about this, because every boy on the team signed this petition."

Suddenly Archie's hand shot up. "I'm Archie Andrews, the captain of the team," he said when Mrs. Van Nest called on him. "And every boy *didn't* sign that petition." The board members looked puzzled. I saw Reggie glare at Archie. "Jughead Jones, one of our team members, didn't sign that petition. He believes Betty really belongs on our team."

I looked at Archie. He glanced at me and took a deep breath. "In fact," he continued, "I now believe the same thing. I would like to have my name removed from that petition."

I heard Midge whisper, "Way to go, Archie." My mom smiled and nudged me with her elbow. The rest of the boys fidgeted restlessly in their seats. I felt so happy I almost cried.

"You'd like me to take your name off the petition?" Mrs. Van Nest asked Archie.

"Yes, please!" said Archie without a moment's hesitation. He sat back down.

An instant later Chuck's hand shot up. He was recognized.

"My name is Chuck Clayton, and I'd like my name removed from the petition, too, please," he said.

I looked over at Nancy. She smiled and gave me a thumbs-up. Up went Moose's hand, then Dilton's. One by one, almost everyone on the team asked to be removed from the petition. Of course, Reggie and the Turner twins refused to change their opinions. But what they thought didn't matter anymore.

"It seems that we no longer have much of a petition to consider," Mrs. Van Nest announced. She looked at the board members. "All in favor of allowing Betty Cooper to remain on the baseball team, please raise your hands." All of the members raised their hands. The audience cheered. Miss Grundy hugged me. Coach Clayton and my dad shook hands. "It looks like you're back on the baseball team for good, Betty," Mrs. Van Nest said, looking in my direction.

Suddenly I was mobbed by all my girlfriends.

"Congratulations, Betty," said Bernadette. Melanie and Arabella patted me on the back. I saw Moose and Midge and Chuck and Nancy together in the crowd.

"I'm so happy for you," Ronnie said, giving me a kiss on the cheek. "But now I've got to run. The meeting was short, so if I hurry I still might be able to keep my manicure appointment." She smiled and rushed off.

I looked over to where the boys had been sitting. I saw Reggie stomp out of the room, followed by the Turner twins. But I didn't see Archie.

"Welcome to the team, Betty," said Dilton, coming over to me with Luis.

"Thanks, Dilton," I replied. "Have you seen Archie?"

"He left as soon as the board voted," Luis answered.

"Oh," I said. I went back to accepting the congratulations of my friends—but I was disappointed that Archie was gone. It was Archie who had gotten the ball rolling by standing up and admitting he had been wrong about me.

Chapter 10

"It's been quite a night," my mom said as we walked toward our station wagon. We'd finally managed to sneak out of the auditorium. I'd spent the previous twenty minutes accepting the congratulations of everyone from Mrs. Van Nest and Superintendent Harper to Arabella and Moose.

"I'm glad everything worked out," my dad said. "There should be no more trouble about this baseball thing now."

"I wouldn't count on that, Dad," I said. "You should have seen Reggie's face when he stormed out of the building."

"I wouldn't worry about Reggie," someone said from the shadow of a huge oak. We stopped and turned toward the nearby tree. "Reggie will get over this," said Archie, stepping out of the darkness.

"Archie!" I exclaimed as he walked up to us.

"I've been waiting for you to come out," he said.

"Thank you for what you said at the meeting, Archie," I told him.

Archie shook his head. "There's no need to thank me," he answered. "I finally came to my senses and did the right thing. A lot of us have been acting like real jerks."

"Let's forget about what happened and concentrate on what's going to happen from now on," I replied.

"Sounds good to me," Archie agreed. He looked at my parents. "Is it okay if the captain of the team drives one of the players home?" he asked them.

"If it's okay with Betty, it's fine with us," my mom answered.

"It's about time things around here got back to normal," my dad added. Archie's recent absence from our home had really seemed strange to him.

"Thanks, Mom and Dad," I said. I dashed up and kissed them both.

My parents said good night to Archie and walked off.

"Ol' Betsy is parked over here," Archie said, taking my hand. It felt good to be holding hands with Archie again. "I've missed you," he said.

"I missed you, too," I admitted. I laughed. "I never thought baseball would be the thing to come between us."

"Me, either," Archie chuckled as we got in his jalopy.

"I always thought it would be Veronica," I kidded.

"Speaking of Veronica, I guess now she'll start talking to me again," said Archie. He put the key in the ignition. Ol' Betsy rumbled, shook, and backfired loudly. The motor wheezed and then kicked over. Archie put Ol' Betsy into gear, and away we chugged.

"Do you really think Reggie will get over this?" I asked.

"He'd better," Archie said. "Our first game is next

week. We'll have to pull together as a team if we want a shot at the championship."

I nodded. "Is Southside really that good?"

"Al Zimmerman makes them good," Archie replied. "He's why they're the defending champions. He already holds the state record for career strike-outs!"

"Is he faster than Big Moose?" I asked. I couldn't believe any high-school pitcher could throw harder than Moose.

"They don't call him Zippy for nothing," Archie replied. "I've heard he's been timed at ninety-four miles an hour."

I whistled. "I guess beating them won't be easy," I commented.

"It'll be tough," Archie agreed. "Zippy is not only a good pitcher, he's a real competitor. He takes base-ball even more seriously than I do. I guess he figures he'll turn pro right after high school. He has a great chance of being drafted by a pro team."

"What about college?" I asked Archie.

"Zippy isn't much of a student," Archie answered. "He lives to play baseball. And he's not really the nicest guy, either. His personality is in his throwing arm."

The traffic light changed from yellow to red. Ol' Betsy rumbled to a stop. "You sound like you don't care for him," I said as I bounced in my seat. Ol' Betsy was *not* the smoothest-running car in River-dale.

"I don't," Archie said. "I respect him as a player, but otherwise I can't stand him. He's a braggart and a sore loser." Archie shrugged. "Wait until we play Southside. You'll see what I mean."

The light changed again. We rumbled off toward my house. "I'd ask you out for pizza or something, but I promised my dad I'd go right home after the meeting," Archie said.

"It's okay," I answered. "I'm kind of tired anyway. It's been a long day."

Archie pulled up in front of my house.

"Thanks for the ride," I told Archie.

He looked me in the eyes. "It was my pleasure."

Slowly our faces came together. Our eyes shut and our lips touched. We kissed. It was nice. I had missed Archie a lot.

"Good-bye, Archie," I said after our lips parted.

"Bye," Archie answered. "See you tomorrow at practice. In fact, I'll pick you up on my way there, if you need a lift."

"I sure do," I answered, sliding across the seat and opening the door.

"See you then," Archie called.

I waved good-bye and walked toward the house. Tomorrow's practice was the last one before the start of the season. I couldn't wait for our first game.

Chapter 11

We crowded around Coach Clayton in the dugout. The visiting team was practicing in the infield. I couldn't help but feel excited. The weather was perfect for the opening game of the season, against Pine Ridge High School. I was dressed in my brand-new baseball uniform. And even though I was just a sub— and would probably spend the entire game on the bench—I was ready to play ball. Dilton was slated to start at shortstop, and deservedly so.

"Okay, Riverdale," said Coach Clayton. "I know we're going to have a successful season." He looked out at the field. "We're as good as any team in the league. Let's go out and show Pine Ridge what we've got!"

We all cheered and then broke from the huddle. Some of the players walked out of the dugout to toss a ball around. Our starting pitcher, Chuck, was already warming up with Freddie, our catcher. Big Moose wasn't scheduled to throw on opening day. Coach Clayton was saving him to pitch against Southside High, three days from now.

I walked out of the dugout to ask Archie about some of Coach's signals. As I stepped onto the field,

I saw three boys I didn't know, standing on the other side of the fence. I thought they were just regular spectators—until I noticed they were wearing Southside High varsity jackets.

"Look!" said the big burly boy with short dark hair. "It's true! They do have a babe on their team! What a hoot!" The three of them began to laugh.

I got mad but tried not to show it. I bit my lip and slowly headed for Archie.

"At least she isn't a dog," the boy continued. "In fact, Blondie is kind of cute. She can manage our team if she ever gets tired of playing with these wimpy losers."

"Who's that big jerk?" I said when I finally reached Archie.

Archie held the ball he'd been tossing with Jughead. "That jerk is Zippy Zimmerman, Southside's all-state pitcher," Archie answered me. "He's quite a charmer, isn't he?"

I looked back over my shoulder at the three Southside players. "What are they doing here?" I asked.

Jughead spoke up. "Southside's season doesn't open until tomorrow," he explained. "I guess they finished practice early today and came over here to scout our team for Friday's game."

At that moment Coach Clayton called us back into the dugout. The umpire had arrived, and it was time for the game to start.

"Hey, Al, are you pitching against us on Friday?" Archie asked Zimmerman as we walked by.

"I sure am, Andrews," Zimmerman replied. "Who's going to pitch for your team—Blondie over there?" He pointed at me as he and his friends laughed loudly.

"Great," Reggie groaned, coming into the dugout. "We haven't played a single inning yet, and already we're the laughingstock of the league. I knew this would happen."

"Can it, Reggie," Luis said. He sat down on the bench.

"Okay, Riverdale," said Coach Clayton. "Take the field and bring home the win."

The starters ran onto the field and took their positions—Moose at first, Archie at second. Dilton was the shortstop, and Reggie was the third baseman. The outfield consisted of Jughead, Luis, and Eddie. Chuck was the pitcher, and Freddie was the catcher.

"Go get 'em, guys!" I shouted. I clapped and cheered with the rest of the players on the bench.

"Play ball! Batter up!" the umpire yelled as he pulled his mask down over his face.

"Show them what you've got, Chuck," I shouted to our pitcher. "Let's go, Riverdale! Let's have three fast outs!"

Chuck's first and second pitches were balls. He seemed to be having trouble with his control. He walked the lead-off batter on four straight pitches—a bad start for our team.

Then Chuck settled down. He struck out the next batter, but the runner on first advanced to second when Freddie dropped one of the pitches.

With one out, the runner moved to third when another pitch got away from Freddie. The next batter hit a deep fly to the right field. Jughead caught it, but the runner on third tagged up and scored Pine Ridge's first run of the game. Jug never had a chance to throw him out.

The next batter hit a sharp grounder to second base. Archie stabbed the ball and fired it to Moose for out number three.

The team jogged into the dugout. "Let's get it back, guys," Archie encouraged.

"We can do it," I called. "Let's go!"

Dilton led off the inning by hitting a ball at the Pine Ridge third baseman. The fielder bobbled the ball, and Dilton was safe on an error. Luis batted next and struck out.

Archie stepped up to the plate. He belted the first pitch right up the middle for a base hit. Dilton was held at second.

Big Moose walked to the plate. He took the first two pitches. One was a ball; the other was a called strike. He drilled the next pitch into left center field. Dilton rounded third and headed for home as the Pine Ridge left fielder chased down the ball. Dilton scored! The game was now 1–1. Archie rounded third base, and Coach Clayton waved him home. Then the left fielder threw the ball to the infield. The relay throw from the shortstop to the catcher was perfect, and Archie was tagged out at home. Moose stopped at second.

Chuck was the next batter. He struck out to end the first inning.

"This is going to be a close game," Archie said. He picked up his glove. "We're going to have to hustle to beat this team."

The game stayed close for the next five innings. Pine Ridge scored twice, but so did we. Going into the seventh and final inning of the game, the score was tied at three. Chuck had settled down and was still pitching. He was scheduled to face the middle of the Pine Ridge batting order.

"Let's go, Chuck!" I yelled as the Pine Ridge hitter stepped into the batter's box. He swung at the first pitch and smacked a sizzling liner into the gap between third and shortstop. Dilton got a good jump on the ball and managed to make a great backhanded stop. But as he turned to throw to first base, he twisted his ankle and crumpled to the ground before he could release the ball. With the runner safe on first, time was called. Coach Clayton ran out onto the field. I stood by the bench and watched Coach examine Dilton's ankle. It was obvious that Dilton was in pain. Coach Clayton signaled for Bill Morgan to come and help him carry Dilton into the dugout.

"Get your glove, Betty," Coach Clayton instructed me as he helped Dilton onto the bench. "You're in the game."

I nodded. "Yes, Coach." I grabbed my glove and ran out. The players on the Pine Ridge team actually laughed as I took the field. I paid no attention to them as I took my warm-up throws.

"Stay loose now, Betty," Archie called from second base. "There's a man on and no outs!"

"Right!" I called back. I looked to my right, over at Reggie at third. He just turned away from me without saying a word.

"Play ball!" the umpire shouted. Up stepped the

next batter. I got in a ready position. I'd played too much ball over the years to be nervous.

Chuck began his windup. After getting the batter to swing at his first pitch, Chuck threw four straight balls, walking him. That put runners on first and second with no outs. It was the last inning and the score was tied. If either of those runners crossed the plate, we'd be in real trouble.

Chuck wiped the sweat from his forehead. He knew he had to get the next batter, and he did—he struck him out on an excellent curve ball.

"One down," Archie shouted.

"One out!" I called to the outfield.

Chuck threw a fast ball down the middle to the next batter. The guy swung and hit a line-drive rocket right to me. I caught the ball on the fly, then looked toward second. The runner was off the base and surprised by my catch. I fired to Archie, who raced to second base. Archie caught the ball and tagged the sack to complete the double play.

"Laugh that off, Pine Ridge," I said to myself.

"Three outs!" the umpire yelled.

"Great play, Betty!" shouted Archie. He ran over and patted me on the back.

"Way to go, Betty," Coach Clayton called.

"Nice catch, Betty!" Freddie shouted from behind the plate. I smiled. It was the first nice thing Freddie had said to me since I'd joined the team.

"How's your ankle?" I said as I walked up to where Dilton was sitting.

"Sore," he answered. "Nice play, Betty. Now get a hit so we can win this game. I want to go home and soak my ankle."

I walked out of the dugout and put on a helmet. Then I picked up my bat and waited for the pitcher to finish his warm-up throws. I was the first batter up.

"Remember, we need you on base," Coach Clayton said.

Since the score was tied and it was the bottom half of the last inning, we needed only one run to win the game.

"Batter," called the umpire. I stepped into the box.

"Give the ball a ride, sweetie," I heard Zimmerman shout from the fence. "Don't be afraid of the ball. It won't hurt you, honey."

I ignored the remarks from the stands and concentrated on the pitcher. I didn't swing at the first pitch. It crossed the corner of the plate for a called strike.

"Wasn't that good enough for you, babe?" the catcher cracked as he threw the ball back.

I didn't answer. I just dug in with my back foot and got ready to hit.

"You can do it, Betty!" I heard Jughead yell.

"Now you're ready," Archie shouted.

The next pitch was a fastball down the middle. I swung and connected. *Crack!* The ball sailed into right center field, hit the turf, and skipped all the way to the fence.

I took off like a shot. I passed first and rounded second. The ball was thrown into the infield just as I slid safely into third.

The guys in the dugout went wild, jumping up and down and cheering. Coach Clayton, our third base coach, gave me a high five. "No outs," he said. "Don't take any chances. You're the winning run."

I nodded as Luis stepped up to hit. The Pine Ridge pitcher was so rattled that he walked Luis. Archie stepped up.

"Hit me home, Archie!" I shouted, clapping my hands.

The first pitch to Archie was outside. The pitcher fired again. Archie swung. *Crack!* He walloped a line drive up the middle and I trotted home to score the winning run. Archie touched first base. The game was over.

The whole team raced out of the dugout to congratulate Archie and me. Even Dilton hobbled out.

"Way to do it!" the guys said to me as they gave me high fives. I even got high fives from the Turner twins, Tom and Bill. Reggie's regiment of Guys Against Girl Baseball Players had spontaneously disbanded. I was finally an official teammate.

Only Reggie seemed reluctant to offer me his congratulations. He commented, "Nice hit," but it seemed flat and unenthusiastic.

"We're on our way, Betty," Archie said, shaking my hand. "We've got win number one under our belts."

I looked toward the rail behind the dugout, where Zimmerman and his friends were walking away. "Southside High is next on the list," I predicted.

"Definitely," Jughead agreed.

Chapter 12

We sat quietly in the visitors dugout at Southside High and watched Coach Clayton pace back and forth. Out on the diamond were the Southside Seahawks, with Zippy Zimmerman warming up on the mound.

"Southside is the toughest team on our schedule," Coach said. "You've played and practiced well this week. I know you're ready for this big game. I believe we can beat the Seahawks."

Dilton stood up, his right foot in a cast. He had fractured his ankle and would be out for the rest of the season. "We can beat them!" Dilton said. "If you believe it, we can do it! Big Moose is as good a pitcher as Zimmerman, and overall we're a better team."

"I believe we can beat them!" Archie said. He stood up beside Dilton. He raised a fist to the air. "Believe it!" he repeated.

"We believe it!" the Turner twins called as they got up.

Suddenly the entire team started to chant. "We believe it! We believe it! We believe it!"

Coach Clayton waved his hand to quiet us down.

"Now that you believe it, make *them* believe it," he said, pointing at the Southside team. "Do it, Riverdale."

We all cheered. When the team settled down, Archie, Luis, and I went out to take some practice swings. We put on our helmets and selected the bats we wanted.

"Don't let Zimmerman intimidate you," Archie advised as we waited for the umpire to start the game. "He's really not much faster than Moose. You've hit Moose in practice, and you can hit Zimmerman."

I nodded. I looked out at the opposing team. During our warm-ups, the Seahawks had laughed and made a few wisecracks to me, egged on by Zimmerman himself. I just ignored their comments, but some of our players had come to my defense with smart remarks of their own, directed at the Southside squad. The exchange didn't get out of hand, but it was obvious that there was no love lost between Riverdale and Southside. The game was certain to be a hard-fought contest.

"Let's have a batter!" the umpire called.

"Start us off with a hit, Betty," Luis called. I took my place in the batter's box.

"Throw it right by her, Zippy," the catcher called from his crouched position. I got into my stance. Zimmerman went into his windup. The ball whizzed by me and into the catcher's glove before I even got a good look at it.

"Strike one!" the umpire shouted.

"That was his slow-speed change-up pitch," the

catcher said to me as he tossed the ball back to Zimmerman.

I paid no attention to him and got ready to hit. The next pitch was so fast it seemed to leave a vapor trail behind as it jetted toward the plate. I swung and missed. "Strike two!" the umpire called.

I gritted my teeth. I was determined not to strike out. I concentrated on the ball as Zimmerman delivered the next pitch. I swung and missed.

"Strike three!" the umpire shouted. "You're out!"

I started back toward the dugout as the Seahawks tossed the ball around. I'd struck out on three straight pitches.

"Welcome to the league, Blondie," I heard Zimmerman say.

"Don't worry about it, Betty," Luis said as we passed. "He's really fast today."

"You'll get him next time," Archie said.

I put down my bat and helmet and went into the dugout. "Zimmerman doesn't have an arm, he has a flamethrower," I heard Chuck say. "His fastball is really smoking."

Zimmerman was firing rockets to the plate. He struck out Luis for the second out. Archie didn't strike out, but he tapped a soft grounder to the second baseman, who flipped the ball to first for out number three.

It was our turn to take the field. "Okay, Moose," I said as I ran out to my position. "Show Southside they don't have the only good pitcher in the state."

Moose smiled and nodded. We tossed the ball

around the infield as Moose warmed up. He looked really strong on the mound. His fastball was blazing, and his curve was working, too. Hitting him would be no easy task for the Southside players.

"Hey, Moose!" yelled Zimmerman from the dugout. "If you throw me one of those fastballs, I'll hit it out of here."

"You've got to *see* it first, pal," Reggie called from third base. I smiled. I wasn't Reggie's only target.

"Just wait until I get up, pal," Zimmerman shouted back to Reggie. Zimmerman batted fourth for the Seahawks.

Unfortunately for Zimmerman, he never got a chance to make good his boast that inning. Moose struck out the first three batters. The game was scoreless at the end of the first inning.

The second inning was almost a carbon copy of the first. Big Moose flied out to center field. Chuck struck out, as did Reggie.

When the Seahawks got up to bat again, all of Zimmerman's big talk couldn't buy him a hit. He grounded out to Archie at second. The next batter got a cheap pop-fly hit to shallow left field. But Moose struck out the next two batters, so the hit was wasted.

"This looks like it's going to be a real pitchers' duel," Archie said as we went into the dugout at the top of the third inning.

"You said it," Chuck agreed.

"At least Zimmerman has stopped shouting out remarks," I said.

"That's because Moose is pitching as well as he

is," Jughead said. "Zimmerman's worried now. He knows he's in a real ball game."

It turned out to be a great ball game. The two opposing pitchers absolutely dominated the game. After giving up that one hit in the second inning, Moose held the Seahawks hitless for the next four.

Zimmerman did even better. He hadn't allowed one batter to reach base. The only players who even managed to put the bat on the ball were Moose, Archie, and Jughead. Moose flied out two more times. Archie grounded out to both sides of the infield, and Juggie grounded out once and flied out another time. The rest of us struck out. I struck out three times in a row. In all my years of playing softball and Little League baseball, that had never happened to me before.

"This is going to be our inning," Coach Clayton urged us on as we came to bat in the top of the seventh and final inning, the score still 0–0. "Zimmerman has a perfect game going up until now, but his luck is going to run out," Coach continued. "We have the top of our order up. We can do it."

"Believe we can do it," Dilton chanted as he looked up from the scorebook he was keeping for Coach Clayton.

"Believe it!" Reggie said.

"Yeah! Believe it!" Chuck shouted. He looked at me. I was up first. "Get on base any way you can, Betty."

"You can do it, Betty," Archie encouraged. "We need you on base."

I nodded. I had an idea. I stepped up to the plate and got into my stance. I took a few practice swings. "Why don't you throw me something fast this time," I taunted Zimmerman.

He smirked. "You asked for it," he called back to me.

"Quit the talking and play ball," the umpire instructed.

Zimmerman went into his windup. He reared back and threw so hard that he was off balance when he landed. As the ball came to me, I didn't try to swing. Instead I bunted the ball the way Miss Grundy had taught me my first year on the softball team.

Slam! The ball thudded off the bat and dropped between the pitcher's mound and third base. I broke from the plate and raced toward first as fast as I could go. I heard my teammates screaming.

Zimmerman scrambled over to the ball. He grabbed it and flung it to first, but I crossed the bag before the first baseman caught the ball.

"Safe!" yelled the first base umpire. Angrily Zimmerman took off his glove and threw it on the ground.

"*Yahoo!*" shouted Archie, bouncing up and down near the dugout. "There goes his perfect game and his no-hitter!"

Not only was Zimmerman's perfect game a thing of the past, but now we had a chance to win the game. The Seahawks coach called time and went out to speak to his pitcher. Zimmerman put his glove back on and nodded as his coach whispered to him.

Luis waited at the plate. He'd seen the sign Coach Clayton had just flashed from the coaching box at third, and so had I. The Southside coach left the field.

"Play ball!" called the umpire. Zimmerman pitched, and Luis laid down a perfect sacrifice bunt. The ball was fielded by Zimmerman, who threw Luis out at first, but I moved safely to second and was now in scoring position.

Zimmerman seemed shaken as Archie stepped to the plate. The two bunts must have affected his concentration, because he walked Archie on four straight pitches. That put runners on first and second with one out. The Southside coach stood up, but Zimmerman waved him back as Moose stepped into the batter's box.

Zimmerman checked the runners and then pitched. Moose took a mighty cut at the ball. *Whack!* It sailed deep into the gap in left center field, where no one could catch it. The ball crashed against the fence.

I raced from second to third, Archie hot on my heels. Coach Clayton waved us on. I turned the corner from third base and headed home. Score! Archie slid in for run number two. Moose got trapped between second and third and was tagged out by the Southside shortstop, but it really didn't matter. We were out in front, 2–0.

"Way to go, Betty," Tom said as I came into the dugout.

Reggie looked at me and forced himself to smile. "Not bad," he said, "for a girl."

I figured it was the closest thing to a compliment I'd get from him.

"Thanks, Reg," I said.

Moose came into the dugout and got a high five from each of us.

At the plate, Chuck was facing a madman on the mound. But Zimmerman kept his temper in check and struck Chuck out.

"Forget it, Chuck," Archie said as the teams changed places. "All we have to do is hold them."

"Three outs are all we need," I encouraged Moose as I went out to shortstop.

"Duh . . . three outs are what we're gonna get," Moose replied confidently. He winked at me and took his place on the mound to face Southside's hitters.

Moose wasted no time. He sent the first batter back to the bench on four pitches. The next hitter grounded out to Chuck at first. That made it two out in the bottom of the last inning. All we needed was one more out to win.

Up to the plate came Zimmerman.

"Throw it right by him, Moose," Reggie called.

"Show him the high hard one, Moose," Archie shouted.

"Give it to him, Moose Baby!" Chuck hollered.

Moose wound up and delivered a searing fastball. Zimmerman swung. He belted a liner into the gap between Archie and Chuck. The ball looked like a sure hit. Archie made a quick move to his left and dove through the air. He snared the ball and held on to it as he landed on his stomach in the dirt.

"Out!" shouted the base umpire.

We all ran over and mobbed Moose on the mound. "We did it!" Coach Clayton shouted. "I knew we could do it!"

"No one is going to beat us now," Archie said as he handed Moose the game ball. We cheered and cheered until we were hoarse.

"We're number one!" we all chanted. "We're number one. Believe it!"

Chapter 13

The music in the Teen Machine Dance Club was blasting as I danced with Archie. Archie and I, along with Moose and Midge and Nancy and Chuck, had gone to the local club on Saturday night to celebrate. The day before, the softball team had clinched the league championship. Our baseball team was only one win away from doing the same thing.

"I knew we could do it," Archie said as we danced. "We have fourteen wins and no losses. We could be the first undefeated baseball team in the history of Riverdale High."

"It happened because we all believed it could happen," I replied, moving in time to the music.

"Now you sound like Dilton." Archie smiled. Dilton's word had caught on and become our team's slogan for the season. "I believe in the power of positive thinking, but I think hard work had something to do with our team's success," Archie said. The music stopped and we started back to our table. "Most important," continued Archie, "we all played as a team from game one. Everyone contributed."

I smiled at Archie. "It's been a great season," I said. "It was a bit rough at the beginning, but I've enjoyed every minute of it." I shook my head. "I just wish that Reggie would accept me as a teammate."

Archie stopped and looked me in the eye. "I'm amazed that he's held a grudge for so long," he said.

I shrugged. "It's not that he's mean to me," I replied. "It's just that he refuses to treat me like a real part of the team."

Archie took my hand. "I guess Reggie will never change from the kid who didn't want girls to play in Little League," he said, "but all the other guys know how much you've contributed to the team's success this year, Betty."

"We sure do," Chuck piped up as we reached the table. "We would have been in big trouble when Dilton got hurt if Betty hadn't been ready to step in."

"The season's not over yet," I said. Our league schedule called for us to play every team twice. Our final game was against Southside High. Southside's only loss had been to us. If they could beat us in the last game of the season, Riverdale and Southside would end up tied for first place.

"What would happen if Southside beat us?" I asked.

"Betty, you've got to believe that they won't," Chuck answered.

"Duh . . . yeah! Believe it!" Moose urged.

"I do!" I insisted. "I'm just curious to know how the league champion would be determined if Southside High somehow managed to beat us."

Suddenly a couple pushed through the crowd behind us. "Did I hear someone mention Southside High School?" It was Zimmerman. He smiled as he

glanced around our table. "What is this?" he asked as he winked at his girlfriend. "It can't be a victory celebration. You haven't beaten us yet."

"How are you doing, Al?" Archie said. The boys made introductions all around.

"I'll be doing better after we beat you guys on Monday afternoon," Zimmerman finally said in response to Archie's greeting. He looked at Moose. "Are you pitching on Monday, Moose?" he asked.

"Yup," answered Moose. "Are you?"

Zimmerman nodded. "Of course," he said, "I've got to get revenge for that loss. It's the only one I've had in three years."

"Maybe you'll have another after Monday," I teased.

Zimmerman laughed. "Did you hear that, Alice?" he said. "Isn't Betty a riot? She's the girl I told you about. She plays shortstop on the Riverdale baseball team."

"Really?" said Alice. She smiled at me. "I read all about you in the newspapers." There had been several small follow-up articles about me, after that piece in the season preview. Luckily, though, for the most part I was old news by now. "You're famous," Alice said.

"Not really," I answered. "I just like baseball."

"I like baseball, too," Alice replied. "But I'd never want to play it against boys." She looked at Zimmerman. "Batting against a pitcher like Al would just scare me to death."

"Well, he doesn't scare Betty," Midge answered.

"Not yet," Zimmerman answered. "But just wait

until Monday's game." He grinned at me. "All we have to do is beat you by more than two runs and we retain the league championship."

"Oh! Is that *all* you have to do?" said Nancy, dryly.

"Well, we've got to get back to our table," Zimmerman said. "We have friends waiting."

"Good luck on Monday, Al," Archie said as they started to walk away.

"Yeah, same to you," Zimmerman replied. "You'll need lots of luck to beat us again."

"If they beat us by more than two runs they win the title?" I asked the guys.

"That's right," Chuck answered. "We beat them 2–0 in the first game."

Archie broke in. "If they beat us, we'd be even in wins and losses, so the team that scored the most total runs in the two games would be declared the league champ. That's how the league rules are set up."

I nodded slowly. "I don't think we'll have to worry about that," I said. "After all, we're going to win on Monday."

"Absolutely," Chuck said.

"Duh . . . yeah," Moose agreed.

"I believe it!" Archie assured me. "I believe it!"

Chapter 14

"Look at that crowd," Coach Clayton said to us Monday after school. He pointed toward the stands, packed with our fans. That morning in school, Mr. Weatherbee had made a special announcement over the P.A. system about the game, urging everyone to come out to support us. Students and the Riverdale High staff also were well represented. Mr. Weatherbee and Miss Grundy were on hand—even Mr. Dobson was in the stands. Amazingly, Mr. Dobson had stopped me in the hall during school that day to wish me good luck in the game.

Everyone was excited about the possibility of the baseball and softball teams both winning league championships in the same year. Riverdale High had never accomplished that feat before in its history.

"We're one game away from the title," Coach Clayton said. "There's not much I can say now that I haven't already said this season." He paused. "I just want you to know that no matter what happens on the field today, I'm proud to have coached you all this year."

"I'd like to say something, too," said Archie. He stood up. "Southside High thinks they can beat us.

But I believe they're wrong. We're going to take this championship. What do you think?"

"We believe we can win it!" Reggie yelled.

"We believe it!" Dilton roared.

"We believe!" we all shouted.

"Then go out there and win it, Riverdale!" called Coach Clayton.

We all charged up to our positions. As Moose warmed up on the mound, I could hear Zimmerman talking to his Southside teammates in the visitors dugout.

"The title is ours for the taking," he shouted. "They were lucky the first time they played us. Today we even the score."

We finished our warm-up throws. Reggie tossed the practice ball into the dugout.

"Play ball!" the umpire yelled, summoning the first Southside batter to the plate.

"Okay, Moose. Just like before," I shouted as I got into a ready position.

"Mow 'em down, Moose," Archie coaxed from second base.

Moose's fastball was really humming, but his control seemed off. His first pitch was way outside. His next pitch was also a ball. He walked the first batter.

"Shake it off, Moose," Reggie called.

Moose nodded. He prepared to deliver his first pitch to the next batter. He threw a curve that the batter hit sharply to Archie at second base.

As soon as the ball was hit, I bolted toward the bag at second to cover. Archie flipped me the ball as the Southside runner slid in hard, trying to prevent me from making a double play. I touched the base and fired to first as the runner knocked me flying. My throw was good and I got the out at first, but I landed hard on the infield dirt.

"Hey!" I heard Reggie yell to the runner. "Watch that stuff!"

"Tough!" the runner said. He got up and trotted off. "If she can't take it, get her off the field!"

"She can take it!" Reggie responded. He helped me to my feet. "Are you okay, Betty?"

I dusted myself off. "Yeah, Reg, thanks. And I do mean thanks!"

"Are you all right, shortstop?" the ump asked me.

"I'm fine," I answered.

"Let's beat these guys," Reggie said to me.

"Let's," I replied as we both got back into position. I'd never felt more ready to play in my life.

"Duh . . . okay, Betty?" Moose called from the mound.

I nodded to Moose and looked toward the plate. Obviously Southside had changed its lineup a bit since we'd last faced them. Al Zimmerman was now batting third instead of fourth. "Strike this guy out, Moose," I called.

Moose went into his windup and then fired a blazing fastball toward the plate. Zimmerman swung, *Crack!* The ball jumped off the bat and flew deep into the outfield. All we could do was watch as the ball cleared the fence for a home run.

Zimmerman chuckled as he circled the bases. "That's the first run of many," he said as he passed me on his way to third.

"It's early," I said. "The game is a long way from over!" Zimmerman just laughed and kept moving. When he touched home, he was mobbed by his team.

"Don't let it bother you, Moose," Chuck shouted. "We'll get it back."

Moose nodded. He took a deep breath and concentrated on the next batter. He struggled a bit but managed to get the hitter to strike out.

"Moose doesn't seem to have it today," Archie said as we ran off the field together.

"Maybe he's just nervous," I answered. "He'll settle down."

Archie nodded. We went into the dugout down by a run.

Luis, Archie, and I collected our helmets and bats. "It's Riverdale's turn to score," Dilton said.

"Start us off right, Betty," Reggie urged.

I smiled at Reggie. He seemed different. I guess he really wanted to win that championship.

The crowd roared as I stepped up to the plate. "Sock it, Betty!" Midge yelled from the stands. I saw Midge sitting with Nancy, Melanie, and Ronnie. Ronnie was busy filing her nails and not paying any attention to the game. But at least she was there.

I got into the batter's box. Zimmerman took his catcher's sign and nodded. He went into his windup. The first pitch was a belt-high fastball that zoomed by me for a strike.

I gritted my teeth and took a practice swing. I was determined not to strike out. He pitched again. I swung hard but managed only to tap a soft roller back to Zimmerman on the mound. He fielded it easily and waited for me to run most of the way to first before tossing the ball to the first baseman for the out.

"Nice try, Betty," Jughead said. He was nibbling on a candy bar in the dugout. I sat down beside him. We watched as Luis popped out to first for out number two. Archie singled next to left field. But he ended up out at second when Moose hit into a force play.

"This is going to be our toughest game yet," Jug said as he finished his candy bar. He picked up his glove. "Zimmerman will be hard to beat, now that his team has the lead."

"We'll see if he can keep that lead," I said. We got up and raced out to our positions on the field.

Southside not only kept the lead but added to it. In the third inning, they got another run on an error by Eddie and a double by the Southside catcher. As the game wore on, it became obvious that Moose was very vulnerable on the mound. In the fifth inning, he walked the first two batters. Zimmerman then got up and cracked a double to right—another run. That made it 3–0 in favor of Southside High. When Moose walked the next batter to load the bases, Coach Clayton called time-out. Everyone knew a pitching change was in order. Moose and Chuck swapped positions. The crowd applauded as Moose walked over to first.

"It looks like we're going to remain the defending champions, doesn't it?" Zimmerman taunted Archie as Chuck warmed up.

"That guy is more obnoxious than I am," Reggie muttered to me. He pointed at Zimmerman.

"You're not obnoxious," I reassured Reggie. "You just have distorted views on certain issues."

Reggie smiled good-naturedly.

"Batter up!" called the umpire when Chuck was ready to pitch.

The first batter singled sharply to right field. Jughead fielded the ball quickly and threw it in, so only one run scored. That put Zimmerman on third. We were losing 4–0, and the bases were still loaded with no outs.

"Move the infield in," Coach Clayton shouted. "Make the force play at home. We can't afford to give up any more runs."

We infielders moved up onto the grass. Chuck pitched. The ball was hit to me. I fielded it and fired the ball home to Freddie. He caught the ball and stepped on the plate just as Zimmerman slid right into him. He knocked Freddie over but didn't jar the ball out of Freddie's glove.

"*Out!*" called the home plate umpire. Zimmerman got up and angrily stomped off toward the dugout.

"One down," yelled Archie. "Let's get two!"

The next play was even better. The batter grounded to Archie. Archie tagged the Southside runner going to second and then fired to Moose at first for out number three.

"Now let's get some runs," Chuck called as we ran in.

"Start us off, Moose," Dilton shouted as he looked up from the scorebook.

Moose nodded. He put on a helmet and picked up a bat.

After Zimmerman warmed up, Moose stepped into

the batter's box. He had a determined look on his face as Zimmerman delivered the ball. *Crack!* Moose smashed a towering fly ball that sailed over the fence in deep center field for a home run. Zimmerman kicked dirt on the mound as Moose circled the bases. The crowd roared and chanted, *"Moose! Moose! Moose!"* We all lined up at home and high-fived him as he crossed the plate.

"Duh . . . that's one!" Moose said. "All we need are four more!"

Those four more runs proved hard to come by. Even though Freddie singled in the inning, we just couldn't knock him in. The fifth inning ended with the score 4–1.

At the end of the sixth, the score was still the same. Zimmerman and Southside seemed to be in control of our destiny. When we came into the dugout for the last half of the seventh and final inning, things looked bleak. The top of the order was up for us, but we needed three runs to tie and four to win. It would be a difficult task.

"If we don't get some runs, we're going to lose the championship," Archie said to the team as Zimmerman warmed up.

"We can do it!" Jughead said. "Our best hitters are up."

Dilton stood up and wobbled a bit because of the cast on his foot. All he said was one word. "Believe."

"Batter," called the umpire.

"I believe," I said to the team as I went out to hit. The crowd roared.

"Come on, Betty!" shouted Miss Grundy.

"Get a hit, Betty!" Melanie shouted.

"Betty Cooper, if you don't do something good, I'll never speak to you again!" Veronica shouted.

I stepped up to the plate and cocked my bat. I saw a smug look on Zimmerman's face. The only hit I'd gotten off him in our two games was that bunt single. "Give it your best shot, Zippy!" I said softly to myself. He pitched. I swung. *Crack!* I hit a shot into left center field. The ball hit the grass and skidded to the fence. I dropped my bat and raced to first. I didn't stop running until I was standing safely on second. The crowd clapped wildly.

Luis stepped up to bat. The first pitch was a ball. I saw him dig in at the plate. The next pitch was a fastball. *Crack!* Luis belted it over the head of the second baseman and into right field. I raced for third, rounded the bag, and headed for home. I crossed the plate standing up as Luis scooted into second.

"Yeah, Betty!" called Reggie, slapping my hand. He made me feel so good I could have hugged him. All the other players congratulated me, too. Our fans were going out of control.

I sat down near Jug to watch Archie hit. The score was now 4–2. The championship hung in the balance.

Archie swung at the first pitch and missed. He stepped out of the batter's box and took a deep breath before stepping back in. He readied himself for Zimmerman's next pitch. *Thwack!* He swung and connected. The ball rocketed off his bat toward the left field fence.

"Get out of here, ball!" I yelled, jumping up. Everyone on the bench did the same. The ball cleared the fence for a home run. We went wild.

When Luis and Archie crossed the plate, we were all waiting outside the batter's box to congratulate them.

"You did it, Archie!" I yelled. I was so happy, I felt like kissing him. But I didn't think it would be good sportsmanship for the shortstop to kiss the second baseman during the game, so I resisted.

The score was tied at four as Big Moose strolled to the plate. He stepped in the box and took some practice swings.

"Be patient, Moose," Coach Clayton called. "Wait for a good one."

On the mound, Zimmerman looked mad enough to explode. "Wait for a good one," Coach repeated. Zimmerman threw the fastest pitch I'd ever seen. It must have looked good to Moose, because he wasn't patient. He swung with all his might. *Whack!* The noise of the bat meeting the ball sounded like the crack of thunder. There was no doubt where that ball was going. It sailed out of the infield, over the fence, and out of the stadium for a game-winning home run. As Moose circled the bases in triumph, the Southside Seahawks left the field in disgust.

"We won it! We won it!" Chuck Clayton shouted.

"We're the champions!" Reggie cried. He and the rest of the team raced out to greet Moose at the plate.

"We won! We're the champions!" Dilton cried.

The Riverdale fans poured out of the stands and onto the field. It was chaos! It was mayhem! It was wonderful!

"We're the champions, Betty!" Archie said, hugging me. He was bubbling with excitement. "We did it! We are the champions!" And then he did something I hadn't dared to do. Riverdale's second baseman gave Riverdale's shortstop a big congratulations kiss.

Chapter 15

I proudly sat with my parents at the end-of-the-year Riverdale High Baseball Banquet. Seated with us were Archie and his folks and Reggie and his mom. Reggie's dad was away on business.

"That's a nice trophy," my dad said, admiring the baseball trophy in front of me.

Every member of our team had a similar trophy. After the dinner, Coach Clayton had spoken about our undefeated season and our league title. He had then presented the huge league championship trophy to Mr. Weatherbee to be placed in the school's trophy case. After Mr. Weatherbee had accepted the trophy, he announced a surprise gift donated by the members of the school board. Each member of the baseball team was given a trophy to commemorate our undefeated season.

"I'm more proud of this," I said, holding up the varsity letter that Coach Clayton had awarded to me prior to the trophy presentation. Four boys and I had won our first baseball letters that year.

"You certainly earned that letter," my mom said.

"Now it's time for the special awards," Coach Clayton continued. "The team has voted for next year's

captain and for this year's most valuable player."

"I voted for you for captain, Archie," I whispered across the table.

"I didn't," Reggie said.

"We know," Archie kidded. "You always vote for yourself, Reggie."

"Of course," Reggie replied. "Like I've told you before, I've never met any player who deserved my vote more than I do."

Archie shook his head. "Well, I voted for Moose," he said.

"There were sixteen players on our team this year," Coach Clayton continued. "Of those sixteen possible votes, Archie Andrews received fourteen votes for captain."

I applauded wildly, as did everyone else.

"Archie will be our captain again next season. Stand up and take a bow, Archie." Coach looked toward our table. Archie stood up and acknowledged the cheers and applause of the crowd. He sat back down.

Coach Clayton picked up the most valuable player trophy. "Now for the MVP Award," he said.

"I voted for Moose," I said to Archie. "How about you?" I didn't bother to ask Reggie about his vote because I knew what his answer would be.

"I'll never tell," replied Archie, smiling from ear to ear.

"This award was almost unanimous," Coach Clayton said. "Almost everyone agreed on our most valuable player for this season. The winner got fifteen out of sixteen possible votes." He looked over at our

table and stared right at me. "This year's most valuable player on the Riverdale baseball team
is . . . Betty Cooper!"

Everyone started to clap. I was too shocked to
move. Reggie and Archie whistled and hooted.
Slowly my father helped me out of my seat. For a
second I just stood there, staring at Reggie. How
could I have gotten fifteen out of sixteen votes when
I voted for Moose, and Reggie always voted for himself? The vote count had to mean that . . .

"Reggie—" I began.

"I told you I'd never met any player who deserved
my vote more than I did . . . until this year!" Reggie
explained. He smiled and winked at me. "Now go
get your award. You've earned it . . . Betty Cooper—
Baseball Star!"